"No! It can't be!

Sara's mind began to whirl with her confusing thoughts. Dathan dead. How was it possible? Surely God had a purpose for his life. He couldn't die this young, he just couldn't. Feelings of guilt overwhelmed her. She hadn't been the kind of sister she should have been, and truth to tell, she had loved Decimus more than her own brother.

Now she could never make it up to him, never ask his forgiveness. She felt somehow to blame. Staring into the intense blue eyes in front of her, she felt her anger begin to boil. Hadn't she told Antonius that Dathan was just a boy? He couldn't be expected to survive such harsh conditions as the galleys.

Black anger clouded her reasoning as she continued to stare at Antonius. He was to blame. He was the one who had put these things into motion and brought such a disaster upon her brother.

"It's your fault," she told him tonelessly.

Antonius released her hands, drawing back at the pain she inflicted with her words. He had already fought with his own feelings of guilt, his own self-condemnation. But there was more that Sara needed to know. There was more to the story.

"Sara."

"No!" Sara jumped to her feet, almost knocking him to the floor where he was still kneeling. When he reached out to her, she drew back sharply and stared at him with loathing. "You killed him. You murdered him!"

DARLENE MINDRUP is a full-time homemaker and home school teacher. A "radical feminist" turned "radical Christian," Darlene lives in Arizona with her husband and two children. *The Eagle and the Lamb* is her first published novel. She believes "romance is for everyone, not just the young and beautiful."

The Eagle and the Lamb

Darlene Mindrup

Heartsong Presents

*To my mother who taught me to be the best
I could be. And to my beloved husband
who believes that I am.*

A note from the Author:
*I love to hear from my readers! You may write to me at
the following address:* **Darlene Mindrup
Author Relations
P.O. Box 719
Uhrichsville, OH 44683**

ISBN 1-57748-008-2

THE EAGLE AND THE LAMB

Cover illustration by Gary Maria.

PRINTED IN THE U.S.A.

prologue

The amazed murmurs of the crowd ascended slowly to a deafening roar. Parthians, Medes, Elamites, Judeans, all chattered and motioned frantically at one another.

Jubal Barjonah pushed himself forward angrily, his eyes coming to rest on the leader of the Galileans. What was his name? Simon, called Peter, that was it.

Twelve of them stood and faced the crowd, but it was Peter who addressed them.

"Ye men of Judea, and all ye that dwell at Jerusalem, be this known unto you, and hearken to my words."

The crowd quieted, their attention focused on the speaker. He continued.

"These are not drunken, as ye suppose, seeing it is but the third hour of the day." Jubal could hear several snickers in the crowd.

"But, this is that which was spoken by the prophet Joel."

Jubal's startled eyes flew to Peter's face, his attention suddenly riveted. Jubal had studied the prophet Joel's writings for many years. He almost had a passion for them. They and the writings of Isaiah were his favorites. Peter's quoting of Joel was totally accurate, but how did that apply to this situation? Jubal's attention was caught once more as the voice went on, vibrant and full of authority.

"Men of Israel, hear these words; Jesus of Nazareth, a man approved of God among you by miracles and by wonders and signs, which God did him in the midst of you, as ye yourselves also know."

There was no denying the man Jesus of whom he spoke

5

was a fantastic magician. Jubal had seen the results of his "healings."

Peter continued. "Him, being delivered by the determinate counsel and foreknowledge of God, ye have taken, and by wicked hands have crucified and slain."

Jubal felt a stab of guilt when he remembered his part in the debacle. He had been one of the crowd shouting for the crucifixion of the man they called Jesus.

As Jubal listened to Peter quoting from the Psalms of David, he felt convicted by the things he had to say. Could it be true what he said? Was it possible that Jesus fulfilled the old prophecies?

Suddenly the writings of Isaiah came clearly to his mind. The false witnesses at the trial, Jesus' refusal to answer the charges. Struck and spit on, and still He did not open his mouth.

Jubal's face paled and his heart started to thunder. What had they done? His mind twisted with the agony until he cried out with the others.

"Men and brethren, what shall we do?"

Peter replied, "Repent, and be baptized every one of you in the name of Jesus Christ for the remission of sins and ye shall receive the gift of the Holy Ghost. For the promise is unto you and to your children, and to all that are afar off, even as many as the Lord our God shall call."

Jubal pushed forward with the frenzied crowd, intent on reaching the speaker. The words of the mighty Joshua came to his mind. From this day forward, he and his house would serve the Lord.

one

The sound of thundering hooves broke the silence of the still, peaceful morning. Two riders appeared on the brow of the hill. Though both were large and strong, one stood out as the more confident of the two. His black hair was cropped close to his head and glistened with the moisture from his perspiration. Bare, muscular arms rippled against the short white tunic he wore so gracefully. Eyes as blue as the Mediterranean gave evidence of his Greek ancestry.

He and his steed matched perfectly. Both large and powerful. One barely under control, hooves stomping in frustration at being held in check.

"Easy, Orion," the rider soothed as he reached down to stroke the horse's neck. "We must remember our friends."

The friend in question quickly caught up, his breathing more labored than his companion.

"For pity's sake, Antonius, can't you control that mangy beast?" he complained in irritation. "I thought we were on a hunt, not having a race."

Antonius glanced at his friend, his eyes roving over his already lathered horse. A fierce pride welled up inside Antonius. Orion was the best horse the Roman legion had to offer, but only because he belonged to Antonius personally.

Since Antonius' father had been a senator and had the ear of the emperor, Antonius had been granted special privileges. Orion was the one Antonius was the most grateful for. Already the stallion from Thrace had been instrumental in saving his life. More than once.

Orion was not lathered at all. Even now, after an hour of riding, it still took all of Antonius' energy to control him. Sliding from his mount, Antonius dropped the reins and stared about him.

"Come now, Flavius. Surely you are not tired."

Flavius dismounted also, brushing dark hair from his eyes. "As though I would admit it if I were."

Antonius grinned, but jerked to attention when he noticed movement from the trees to his left. Motioning Flavius to silence, he reached for his bow and quiver of arrows. A glitter of excitement sparkled in his eyes as he took aim.

"What do you see?" Flavius whispered urgently, trying to peer in the direction Antonius was aiming.

"If I'm not mistaken, there's a deer among those trees. See the brown spot? To the left."

A slight movement caught Flavius' attention. "Shoot, Antonius, before he gets away."

The twang of the bowstring was the only answer Flavius received as Antonius' arrow whistled unerringly towards its target. A small thud was followed by a piercing scream that drained the blood from Antonius' face.

"By the gods!" Flavius whispered. "That sounded like a human scream."

Antonius followed the same direction as his arrow, leaping over rocks and roots. Pushing aside the shrubbery, he noticed a small clearing among the bushes. A small body lay crumpled at the edge of the perimeter.

Laying down his bow and arrow, Antonius went quickly forward, turning the body over when he reached it. A young girl lay unconscious before him, her breathing labored. The arrow had pierced her shoulder and blood was flowing swiftly from the wound.

"Zeus!" Flavius' startled exclamation brought Antonius' eyes to his friend.

"Get my water bag," he snapped.

Flavius disappeared from view, returning a moment later with the bag. Antonius opened the flask and poured water over the girl's wound, gently probing with his fingers.

"I need to pull out the arrow, but I need something to stem the flow of blood first."

Flavius looked helplessly around. "What?"

Reaching down to the hem of his garment, Antonius quickly jerked off a piece of material.

"When I tell you, use this to put pressure on the wound."

Flavius nodded his agreement. Sweat beaded on Antonius' lips and face as he gritted his teeth and got ready to pull the arrow free. It was fortunate that the girl was unaware of anything happening to her.

"Now!"

Antonius jerked the arrow and Flavius pushed the material against the girl's shoulder.

"Be thankful it's only a Jewish girl, Antonius. Otherwise there could be big trouble."

Antonius pulled another strip from his garment to use as a bandage to tie the other piece in place. The girl's color was beginning to alarm him.

"She must be from somewhere close. We need to find her village and find help."

Lifting her gently into his arms, Antonius strode swiftly into the open. A piercing whistle rent the air and Orion lifted his head, his ears perked forward. Another whistle and the stallion threw himself forward, hooves thundering towards Antonius.

"Take her, Flavius, and hand her up to me."

Antonius took the girl into his arms, settling her against his chest. Her head fell backwards against his arm, and her eyes fluttered open momentarily. Dazed brown eyes gazed at him uncomprehendingly. A spark of recognition seemed to light behind her eyes and then faded.

"Who are you?" The whispered croak barely made it past her lips before her eyes closed again. *Thank the deities*, thought Antonius. This was not going to be a pleasant ride.

Flavius lifted Antonius' gear to his own horse and quickly followed. A much used path told them in which direction to head and they quickly came upon a small village. People came to their doors and stared with open hostility at the two Roman soldiers.

A young girl standing at the well turned startled eyes upward as Antonius paused beside her. Sudden fear filled her face and she turned to run.

"Wait!" Antonius commanded, and the girl froze. "I need help."

The girl noticed for the first time the bundle held in his arms. Her eyes widened further, and she stared up at him in horror.

"Is this girl from this village?"

The girl nodded her head, her eyes never leaving the figure of the wounded Jewish girl.

"Take me to her family," Antonius commanded again, and the frightened girl quickly turned to point the way. "I said, take me." Antonius had no time and was in no mood to knock on doors.

Orion picked his way among the main street, shying nervously as a door slammed behind him. The girl reached a house that was slightly larger than the rest he had encountered. From what he knew of the Jews, the owner must be somewhat wealthy. Probably a carpenter or a blacksmith. Antonius felt a moment's disquiet.

Flavius pulled up beside him. "Uh oh. This could be trouble."

Antonius gave him a silencing glance and turned when the door opened at the girl's knock. Another young girl stood in the doorway, her eyes widening in alarm when she saw Antonius and Flavius. The other girl spoke quickly to her, but Antonius couldn't understand what was being said. Turning, the girl fled back down the street from whence they had appeared.

"We need help," Antonius barked. The girl jumped slightly and disappeared from view. A moment later the door opened wider and a large man appeared. His beard was white, which told of his age, but his body was large and powerfully built. *Definitely a smith*, Antonius decided.

"What can I do. . .Sara!" He leaped the distance to Antonius' horse, his hands flailing about helplessly. His eyes glared fiercely up at Antonius, who hastened to explain.

"An accident. My friend and I were hunting. . ." Words suddenly failed him at the look of agony on the old man's face.

Reaching up, he gently took the girl from Antonius' arms.

"Simhah!" he bellowed, and the girl who had answered the door came quickly to his side. Seeing the girl in the old man's arms, Simhah paled.

"Don't just stand there! Make ready a pallet. Get some more water from the well. And have Pisgah run for the healer."

Turning, he strode away without so much as a backward glance. Flavius stepped his mount to Antonius' side.

"Come. Let us leave this accursed place. Her people will take care of her now."

Antonius barely heard him. His eyes were following the old Jew as he disappeared from sight. Whether he liked it or not, he felt compelled to stay. He had to make sure the girl was going to live.

"You go, Flavius. I intend to stay and see this through."

Flavius snorted. "Don't expect gratitude from these people. Like as not, they would just as soon split your throat."

The fierceness returned to Antonius' face. Flavius shook his head. The only time he had ever seen that look on Antonius' face was when he was getting ready to do battle.

"All right," Flavius sighed, "but I stay with you." He looked around him nervously. "I don't trust these people."

Dismounting, both men walked to the door. Flavius hesitated, but Antonius pushed his way forward, ducking his head to enter. When Antonius' eyes adjusted to the dim light, he could make out four figures in the room. There were two sections to the room, which had two floor levels, one about eighteen inches above the ground. It was there they had laid Sara and were bending over her.

The old man turned at their entrance, his shaggy eyebrows ascending towards his still full hairline. Antonius could see the struggle going on within the man before he finally came towards them.

"Shalom."

Antonius nodded his head. "Peace be with you, also."

If the old man was surprised, he certainly didn't show it. Antonius thought that the man would have made a fine general. His bearing was almost regal.

The woman leaning over the girl turned to him in surprise. She rapidly fired her speech at him. He answered her quietly, but with authority. Her lips set in a grim line. Again she attacked him with her words, and again he answered quietly. There was no doubt she didn't like what her husband had to say. Her angry eyes rested on Antonius and Flavius briefly before she turned and addressed the old Jew again. This time when he answered his voice rang with his displeasure.

The old woman rose from her place. "Yes, adon," she told him scathingly.

"Abigail!" He glanced at her angrily, but turned towards the Romans. "Is there something more I can do for you?"

Antonius stepped forward, his eyes going to the girl on the mat. "Her name is Sara?"

The old man nodded, questioning Antonius with his eyes.

Before Antonius could form his next question, another old man arrived. He stopped suddenly, his eyes going wide at the sight of the two soldiers. His wizened face and long side-burns gave him a somewhat comical appearance, similar to a little monkey Antonius had once seen at a bazaar. Sara's father turned to him, motioning towards the still figure on the mat.

Antonius frowned as they began to converse in Aramaic, struggling to follow the words. His ability with the language was very limited since he came in contact with it so seldom. Still, he could understand some of what was being said.

"She will live?" he questioned.

The old wizened Jew glared at him. "It's a good thing you Romans are poor marksmen. A little farther to the left and she would not be alive even now."

"Hold your tongue, old man!" Flavius ordered. "Antonius is one of the finest marksmen in all Rome!"

Wizened brown eyes regarded them curiously. "My mistake," he told them and turned away to rummage in the sack he had brought with him. Pulling herbs from the bag, he concocted a poultice that he placed on the wound.

There was a disturbance at the door, and a young Jewish boy entered, a look of fear contorting his features when he saw the Roman soldiers. There was something vaguely familiar about him to Antonius, but he couldn't quite place him. Ducking his head, the boy turned to leave again.

"Dathan!"

The boy stopped, turning reluctantly towards the old man. He was obviously the son.

"Father."

"Where have you been? We have need of you," the boy's father told him.

"I had things to do."

Antonius watched with interest the sulky expression of the boy and the grim set lips of his father. Lifting a goatskin bag, the old man handed it to the boy. "Go and get some water from the well."

The boy's eyes sparked with anger. "That's woman's work! Send Simhah, or if she can't, send Sara."

The old man threw the goatskin at Dathan, launching into a volley of speech that Antonius had no hope of following. The boy's eyes grew wider and his glance flew to Sara. His face paled. Taking the goatskin, he turned and fled. Straightening his shoulders, the old man turned to Antonius.

"The healer says that Sara's chances are good if she can make it through the night. She has lost a lot of blood, but she is healthy and strong."

Antonius wasn't sure if the old Jew was trying to convince himself more than Antonius. Realizing that there was little he could do and that his help wouldn't be appreciated anyway, he prepared to leave. Fixing the man with an imperative eye he told him, "I will return on the morrow."

All the inhabitants of the room watched in silence as Antonius and Flavius turned to leave. The door shut firmly behind them.

"Whew! I was beginning to wonder if we would get out of there with our lives," Flavius joked.

One dark eyebrow winged upwards as Antonius looked him over.

"Surely a soldier of Rome is not afraid of a few old Jews."

Flavius snorted. "The old healer looked like he might be capable of putting a curse on you. The next time you go, be sure you take your shield with you to protect you from the daggers they throw with their eyes."

Mounting their horses, they wheeled and headed out of the village. Antonius rode silently, his face as black as the thunderclouds that so rarely swept through the region. A tick worked continually in his cheek.

"Come now, Antonius," Flavius cajoled. "For the love of Poseidon, you didn't see the girl. It wasn't your fault."

"I'm a trained soldier. I know better than to launch at a target unless I know what the target is. If I were on the battlefield, it could have been one of my own soldiers." His voice quieted, and Flavius realized that he finally spoke of what truly bothered him. "She couldn't have been any older than Diana."

Flavius regarded him somberly, but said nothing. They rode in silence until they reached the outskirts of the city. Flavius eyed Antonius warily, sensing his dark mood.

"Antonius, come to my house tonight. I know just the thing to cheer you up. I'm having a party. Galvus will be there as well as Lucretius and Ovid." He glanced at Antonius slyly. "Helena will be there also."

Visions of the fiery redhead came to Antonius' mind, as well as pleasurable memories of Helena's flirtatious manner. That she desired Antonius was all too clear, but something held Antonius back. Sometimes he wondered if she was as helpless as she seemed to be. Of course, this brought thoughts of Diana to mind. Frowning, he turned to Flavius.

"No, my friend. Tonight I will spend with Diana."

Eyes filled with understanding, Flavius nodded. "Then this is where we part. Give Diana my. . .I mean tell Diana. . .tell her I said hello," he finally finished in a rush. Saluting, he turned his horse about and headed in the opposite direction.

Antonius' dark mood increased. Orion seemed to sense his reluctance and slowed his steps. Tonight he must face Diana. Tomorrow he must face an angry old Jew and, hopefully, a small Jewish girl. Straightening his shoulders, he kicked Orion's sides and hurried home.

two

Sara awakened to almost stygian darkness. A strong odor of dill filled her nostrils. She was disoriented, so she lay still trying to remember where she was. What she had been doing. Slowly the events of the morning came back to her. Had it all been a dream? Trying to lift herself from the pallet, she felt an excruciating pain in her left shoulder. Moaning, she lay back. At the noise, a figure rose up beside her, almost frightening her senseless.

"Sara?"

The moon slivered a beam through the little window that was beside the door. Her father appeared within its beam, and even in the semidarkness she could see the tiredness of his features.

"What happened?" Sara's voice was little more than a whisper. She stared around the room uncomprehendingly, a frown puckering her brow.

"Praise God!" Jubal went down on his knees, almost weeping with relief. He took Sara's hand gently into his large hands, stroking it gently. "You don't remember?"

The frown deepened as Sara tried to remember. She had been at her favorite hiding place trying to work through some of her problems. The little copse in the woods was where she always went when she had a lot of thinking to do. Then there had been two horsemen. She had been fascinated by their fluid movements on their mounts, never having seen a Roman soldier before. And then the larger of the two had dismounted, and she had leaned closer to see him better.

That's the last thing she could remember.

"I was in the woods and I saw two Romans. Soldiers."

Her father laughed without mirth. "It would seem one of them mistook you for an animal. He shot you with an arrow. Ahaz has been hours attending you. Here, let me light the lamp."

Sara was touched. No one wasted oil at night. It was too precious a commodity. Her father must have been truly worried.

When he had lit the lamp, he brought the stand over and set it beside Sara's mat. He sat down beside her and took her hand once more into his. "You little aton," he told her gently. "You could be dead now because of your stubbornness."

Sara smiled slightly at the familiar term that only her father could use as an endearment. To be likened to a donkey was not usually complimentary.

"I have told you to stay close to the village and especially to stay away from the woods, and still you disobey."

The throbbing in Sara's shoulder intensified, and she moaned again. Her mind was becoming fuzzy with the pain, and she was having a hard time understanding what her father was saying. He leaned closer at the sound.

"Your pain is coming back?" He left her side and went across the room, returning with a bowl. Lifting her head gently, he placed the bowl against her lips. "Drink this," he told her.

Her throat felt parched and she drank greedily.

"Not so much." Pulling the bowl away, he placed it on the floor beside him. He watched as the draught worked its way into her system, and her eyes closed softly. A gentle snore brought a slight smile to his face. As he watched her, his face began to cloud with his thoughts. The Roman said he would return on the morrow. His lips set grimly. Taking the lamp from the stand, he blew it out and felt his way familiarly to his own bed. He frowned. Time enough to deal with that when the situation arrived.

❧

When Sara awakened again, the sun was shining brightly through the little windows of the house. She moved her head slowly, careful not to disturb her shoulder. Her mother was pottering in the kitchen, humming a tune she had heard at cousin Bashan's wedding ceremony. Sara smiled slightly. Her father must have told her mother that Sara was well. At least as well as could be expected.

Slowly glancing around the room, she noticed her father's absence as well as Dathan's. Pisgah came in the door quietly, her eyes going towards Sara's mat. A smile brightened her face.

"My lady! Sara is awake!"

Sara's mother whirled around, her face creasing into a smile at the sight of Sara's lively expression. She dropped the bowl she was holding and came quickly to Sara's side.

"Daughter? How do you feel this morning?" She leaned forward a hand and placed it against Sara's forehead, smiling again. "No fever. Thank God."

Sara reached up with her right hand, taking her mother's hand into her own. They smiled at each other and Abigail wiped a tear from her eye.

"What do we have here?" Sara's father stood in the doorway, a load of wood in his arms. His smile beamed across to Sara. "My little aton is alive and kicking?"

He walked across the room and laid the wood beside the fire pit before coming back to where they stood. Placing an arm around his wife's shoulders, he gave her a slight squeeze. "I told you, Mother, that God would take care of her."

Abigail smiled mistily up at him. "Indeed you did."

"Let's give thanks," he told them, and Sara closed her eyes as her father praised God for caring for her and asked that He continue to be with her. "In Jesus' name. Amen."

The rest of the day Sara lay and watched her mother moving about the house. The connecting door to the shop was open, and she could see her father busily working at the forge. Periodically he would come to the door and smile at her, then return to his business. Sara felt warmed by their love.

Around noon, when Sara thought she would die from boredom, she heard a horse approaching. Not the light donkey hooves of the villagers. This had to be a huge horse, if it fit the sound of the steps. She was just wishing she could get a glimpse of it when the steps stopped outside their door. Sara's mother and father exchanged glances before Abigail hurried to close the front door and then the connecting door to the shop.

Antonius dismounted, smiling wryly when he heard the door close. Looping the reins lightly around a bush, he started for the door. Before he could take more than two steps, the old Jew he had seen yesterday approached him from the side of the house. He said nothing, merely standing there staring at Antonius. There was no expression on his face, nor could Antonius see any in the eyes. He thought again what a fine general the man would make.

"I have come to see Sara," Antonius told him.

"Sara is fine. Except for the healing which will take time."

"I will see for myself." Though Antonius hadn't raised his voice, the man knew nothing short of a full-scale war would deter him from his course. He stood silently, eyeing Antonius warily. Nodding his head, he turned and headed for the front door. Antonius quickly followed him.

Although he was not in uniform, Antonius was a commanding presence. Pisgah's eyes widened as he ducked his head and entered. Seeing her distress, Abigail handed her a jar.

"Go and fetch some water from the well."

The girl fled, glancing furtively over her shoulder.

Antonius' eyes went immediately to the mat in the corner. He could see the girl, Sara, staring at him with curious eyes. There was no fear in her countenance. He walked quickly to her side and stared down at her. Her face was pale, her dark hair matted around her shoulders. Only her large, dark eyes seemed to be alive. Antonius wondered briefly what the girl would look like cleaned and dressed properly, not in the brown color she seemed to favor.

"Hello," Antonius talked softly, afraid of frightening her.

"Shalom," she told him. She stared at him, a slight frown puckering her forehead. "I have seen you somewhere before."

Before he could answer, her father stepped between them. "This is the soldier who shot you."

Antonius frowned at him, but returned his eyes to Sara. "It was an accident. I thought you were a deer. Your brown tunic. . ."

Sara nodded understandingly. "I was in the bushes where I ought not to have been. It was forbidden to me and yet. . .I disobeyed." Her eyes pleaded with her father for forgiveness. His answering look assured Antonius, at least, that he would forgive the girl anything.

It was bad manners to ask, but Antonius was determined to stay, for a while at least. "May I sit?"

Abigail was affronted, but short of being rude she had no choice. Taking a stool, she placed it next to him. Ignoring her outraged look, Antonius placed it closer to Sara. The stool was too little for Antonius' large frame, and he realized that this was done deliberately. Irritated, nevertheless he smiled with charm at Abigail. She blinked her eyes and turned away.

Antonius stared at Sara, his eyes going all over her and returning to her face. "I can hardly believe it." He shook his head wonderingly. "I thought for sure. . ."

Sara smiled gently. "That I would be dead?"

A flush spread across Antonius' face, but he merely nodded. "I have never seen such a quick recovery."

"Jewish healers have much knowledge of the body. They also have a secret weapon."

Antonius knew he was being baited, but he took it anyway. "What is this secret weapon?"

Sara smiled at him. "God."

Antonius leaned back and looked at her wryly. "Which god?"

Sara looked at him with wide, innocent eyes. "There is only one God."

Rather than get into a philosophical discussion with her, Antonius changed the subject. "How many are in your family?"

Smiling knowingly, Sara told him.

"And your brother?" The Roman was searching the room with his eyes and Sara began to feel uneasy. Her mother must be having the same reaction, because Sara could see the knife she was using to cut the vegetables shaking in her hand. Her father had gone back to his workshop, but kept them within sight.

"I know your mother's name is Abigail and yours is Sara and your father's is Adon, but what of your brother?"

"What makes you think that my father's name is Adon?" Sara asked in surprise.

"The day I brought you home, yesterday, I heard your mother call him that."

A hand to her mouth quickly covered Sara's mirth, but her eyes were alight with laughter. Antonius wasn't sure what he had said to cause her response, but the smile made the girl almost pretty.

"I take it I've said something wrong?"

Still smiling, Sara answered. "Adon is a Hebrew word for

master. My mother only uses it when she wants to irritate my father."

"Oh."

"Many Jewish women call their husbands adon or baal."

"And baal means?"

"Lord," she told him and watched his eyebrows lift to his dark hairline. "My father's name is Jubal Barjonah," she told him proudly.

"The way your mother said the word, I assume she didn't mean it as a term of obeisance?"

Sara shook her head. "My father doesn't wish to be called lord or master. He says there is only one Lord and one Master. My mother knows this, but. . ."

"I know. Just to irritate."

Sara nodded.

"And who is this Lord and Master?" Antonius wanted to know.

Antonius and Sara jumped when an urn clattered to the floor. Abigail leaned over to pick up the pot, giving Sara a warning look. The look was not lost on Antonius. His glance flicked from one to the other.

Turning back to Sara, he waited for an answer. Sara's eyes reluctantly met his. She was not ashamed of the answer, but her impetuosity may have endangered her family.

"His name is Jesus," she told him softly.

Sudden comprehension dissolved the rising suspicions in his mind. Christians. He glanced around at each of the occupants. No wonder they were so closed and suspicious. He had heard of the persecution of Christians. As yet it had mainly been local and between the different sects of the Jews. If this man was a Jewish Christian, then most of this village must be also. Many Jews had moved to Ephesus because they could no longer trade with the Jewish community. Christians were as avidly hated by the Jews as they were by the Romans.

Nodding his head, his eyes took one more circuit of the room and returned to Sara. "I told my sister about you. She said she hopes the gods favor you with health." Sara frowned, and he hurried to continue. "I will tell her that your God has done so."

Antonius could tell the girl was beginning to tire, so he got quickly to his feet. Her eyes flew upward to his, and he looked searchingly into them, seeking he knew not what. He realized that even with the animosity of her parents she had shown him nothing but kindness. He also realized that, for awhile, he had been able to forget some of his own troubles. There was something about her. Something soothing. Relaxing.

"I am glad that you are better. I am also very glad that I didn't. . ." He hesitated before turning and striding to the door. He nodded his head to Abigail and Jubal before ducking and disappearing outside.

Sara strained to listen, waiting for the sound of the horse's hooves that would signal his departure. She felt an emptiness as she heard him ride away. Strange. What could a Roman mean to her? Sighing, she drifted off to sleep.

24

It was several weeks before Sara was back to her full strength. Her shoulder still pained her somewhat, but she had healed well. She never returned to the copse in the woods, and the Roman never returned to see her. Looking up at the vivid blue of the sky, Sara had to smile. She swung the empty water bag, glad to take from Pisgah the chore of fetching the water. Of course, Pisgah enjoyed the opportunity to gossip with her friends, but the job itself was a tedious one.

Since the well was on the outskirts of the village, one could easily see the main road from its location. As Sara drew the bucket up, she noticed a column of dust rising from the road in the distance. Roman soldiers. Her heart leaped foolishly in response. She couldn't imagine the Roman coming with a squad of troops. Realizing that it would not be good for her to be caught here, she quickly filled the bag and hurried home.

Her father was grinding a sickle when she peeked her head in his shop. "There's a group of Roman soldiers heading this way. About twenty I would say."

Jubal left his grinding wheel and joined his daughter at the door.

"They're still a ways off."

"Could be passing through," her father told her absently. "Find Dathan."

"Yes, father." Sara hurried to the fields where she found her brother. His tools lay beside him, and he was lying on the ground, staring up at the sky.

"Father wants you," she told him.

Dathan jumped, getting quickly to his feet. "Now what?"

Sara hurried after him, reaching the house only seconds after Dathan. Since her mother was still at the weaving loom, Sara assumed her father hadn't mentioned the soldiers. Still, Jubal came frequently to the living rooms with one excuse or another.

Just when Sara had breathed a sigh of relief, there came a pounding on the door.

three

Jubal glanced around the room before going to the door and opening it. His face paled when he found himself confronting a Roman soldier. Behind the soldier stood several other soldiers, the feathers in their helmets quivering in the breeze.

"Is this the house of Jubal Barjonah?"

"Yes." Jubal looked in confusion from one soldier to another. "What can I do for you?"

Sara felt a lump form in her throat. It must have been because she had told the Roman that they were Christians. Her heart started thumping erratically, sudden fear for her family almost overwhelming her.

Slowly the soldier unrolled a scroll. His eyes quickly surveyed the occupants of the room before he started to read.

"This house and all of its possessions are hereby confiscated in the name of Callus Phibeas, soldier of Rome, in payment of the debt owed to him by one Dathan Barjubal."

Dathan leaped to his feet, his eyes darting to and fro seeking a means of escape. Finding none, he turned pleadingly to his father.

"I didn't mean to!" He fell on his knees before Jubal. "Please!" He glanced up at his father, his voice becoming angry. "It was a trick!"

Until that moment, Jubal had hope that this was some kind of mistake. That hope faded fast in the light of his son's behavior.

"My son, what have you done?" There was no fear in the strong voice, only a desire to know the truth.

Dathan hung his head, his hands clenching and unclenching at his sides. His voice was barely a murmur that Sara had to strain to hear.

"A gambling debt."

A sternness settled over Jubal's visage. He turned to the soldier. "How much?"

The Roman laughed, a mercenary light coming to his eyes. "More than you have, old man."

"How much?"

The smile left the soldier's face at the lack of respect in the old man's attitude. Handing Jubal the document, the soldier smirked when he saw the old Jew pale, his eyes widening in alarm.

"But that's impossible!" Jubal turned to his son. "How is this possible?"

"This property is hereby confiscated and will be sold to pay the debt." The soldier smiled a malicious smile. "Including all the residents and servants of this residence."

The look that passed through Jubal's eyes caused the soldier to step back hastily. Turning, he snapped his fingers. "Take them," he commanded, and the guards moved forward as one.

Sara knew her father would be a match for any two men, but when five fell upon him, she knew he had no hope of winning. Everywhere was chaos. Pisgah and Simhah were being led outside in shackles, fear contorting their features.

Dathan tried to flee, but a huge Roman soldier slammed his fist into the side of Dathan's head, sending him sprawling senseless to the floor. Abigail screamed, clinging to Sara. A soldier reached for Sara, leg irons dangling from his fingers. For the first time, the horror of the moment penetrated her shocked senses. She pushed her mother towards the door.

"Run!" she screamed, pain tearing through her scalp as a soldier grabbed her hair and jerked her backwards. She knew it was useless to fight, but she had to try. The soldier grinned down into her face as another soldier applied the shackle to her ankle.

❧

Sara was led outside where her mother was bent weeping over the prostrate figure of her father. He was bound hand and foot, lying semiconscious on the ground. Blood dripped from his head and his mouth, a large bruise beginning to swell his eye.

Abigail was crying softly, while Dathan moaned, his face buried in his hands. Sara watched helplessly while the soldiers ransacked their home. She began to plead with God for their salvation, never expecting it to come in the form of a tall Roman on a large white horse.

Antonius paused, his brow furrowing. Kicking his horse forward, he pulled to a stop at the entrance to the house just as a tapestry flew out the door, barely missing the horse. Orion reared, and it took all of Antonius' skills as a horseman to stay seated astride the frightened beast. By the time he had regained control, the leader of the soldiers was at his side.

"What goes on here?" Antonius roared with anger, his voice quivering in his wrath.

The soldier paled considerably, his Adam's apple moving rapidly up and down. "Tribune! I'm sorry! We didn't see you here." He tried to take hold of Orion's bridle and the horse lashed out with his teeth, barely missing the man's fingers.

Reaching down to calm the high strung horse, Antonius' eyes circled the yard, coming to rest on Jubal and his family. Sara was gently helping her father to his feet.

"You haven't answered my question, soldier. What is going on here?"

Motioning to Dathan, the soldier explained about the gambling debt. "Since he can't pay it, I have been ordered to confiscate this property and all of its occupants."

Antonius arched an eyebrow. "The debt is that large?"

Handing Antonius the scroll, the soldier waited for permission to continue. Instead, Antonius handed the document back. His gaze rested on Sara a moment, a sudden glitter entering his eyes. Reaching into a bag on his saddle, he pulled out a smaller bag, its contents jingling slightly. He motioned the soldier over and thrust the bag into his hand. The soldier lifted puzzled eyes to Antonius.

"Payment of the debt," Antonius told him.

"Sir?" The soldier was beginning to doubt the Tribune's sanity, but he didn't dare question him further.

"I am buying this property."

Jerking his head up in surprise, the soldier opened his mouth and then closed it again. "But Tribune. . .an auction . . .these are not. . .my orders." He stopped, unable to go on.

"Whose orders?"

"Callus Phibeas."

Antonius stared at him until the soldier dropped his eyes. "Since when has Callus had enough rank to issue orders?"

Flushing angrily, the soldier lifted his head. "It's a signed, legal debt."

"Agreed. And now the debt has been paid," Antonius told him, his voice laced with steel. "Should Callus have any questions, send him to me." The last four words, uttered in such a tone, caused the soldier to swallow hard. As the soldier turned to go, Antonius stopped him.

"Wait. What is your name?"

Lifting his chin, the soldier turned to answer. "Marcus Trajan."

Antonius nodded. "Marcus, see that Dathan is sent to the galleys."

A moan caused Antonius to turn his head. Dathan was on his knees, rocking back and forth in the sand. Sara's pleading brown eyes caught his attention. Tightening his lips, he turned back to Marcus. "You have your orders."

"Yes, Tribune." Still the soldier hesitated. "What of the others?"

"Release them."

Remembering the battle between five of his finest men and the old Jew, Marcus was hesitant. "But. . ."

"I said, release them."

Marcus motioned to the two soldiers nearest him, who hastened to obey. Antonius Severus was a wealthy and powerful nobleman, not to mention a Tribune of Rome's army. Let Callus deal with him, if he had a mind to. As for Marcus, he hoped he never found himself in such a predicament again.

They released all except Dathan, who was still sobbing on his knees in the sand. The soldiers hauled him to his feet and led him screaming away.

Sara felt her heart start to pound when Antonius' eyes fastened on her.

"Get your things together. You're coming with me."

"No!" Jubal stepped forward, placing himself between his daughter and the Roman. His huge hands clenched into fists, but Antonius was unmoved.

"Hear me, Jubal Barjonah. You have a wife to worry about. See to her and leave Sara to me."

Jubal's face turned red with rage, and Antonius knew that if he couldn't calm the man, someone might get killed.

"Listen to me, Jubal, for Abigail and Sara's sake." Antonius could see the old man struggling for control and he continued. "I have need of Sara. I believe she can help me with my sister. I know you are angry about Dathan, but he brought his problems on himself. I will not explain my actions to you in this regard. I am taking Sara with me, but you need have no fear for her safety. I do not beat my slaves."

"It is not beating that concerns me."

Antonius was taken aback by the man's forthrightness. A sardonic smile touched his lips as his eyes raked Sara from head to toe. Sara squirmed under his perusal, feeling like a lamb that was found wanting.

"You have no need to fear on that score, either. I have a preference for voluptuous blondes, not skinny Jews."

Sara felt her anger beginning to rise. Realizing that she was in a precarious position and could further hurt her parents, she swallowed down the hurt the Tribune's words had caused her.

Antonius stared hard at Jubal. "We will speak again, but right now I have more pressing matters to attend to."

Jubal was torn, standing rigidly in front of Antonius. His eyes flashed fire that ignited an answering spark in Antonius'.

"Have it your own way." Antonius snapped his fingers and several of the guards stepped forward.

"Wait!" Sara flung herself forward, laying a pleading hand upon her father's arm. "I will go with him."

Jubal stared into Antonius' face. Not so much as a muscle twitch revealed any of the Roman's thoughts.

"What of us?" Jubal finally managed to ask.

Antonius gazed levelly into Jubal's worried eyes. "This property belongs to me now, as do you." He nodded his head towards Abigail and the servants. "As do they." Sara couldn't miss the note of warning in his voice. "Take care of this property as though it were your own, and if Sara serves me well, someday it will be again."

A puzzled look passed between Sara and her father. Antonius sighed impatiently. He laid a hand on Jubal's shoulder and felt the old man stiffen at his touch.

"I don't want your house or you or your servants. I have plenty of my own. But I have need of her." He nodded his head at Sara. "I promise you I will take care of her and that no harm will come to her while she is with me. He placed his hand on the eagle crest of his shield, the crest that represented Rome. "On my honor as a Roman soldier."

Although Jubal had no faith in Roman soldiers, or their oaths, somehow he believed this one. *He would make a good Jew*, Jubal thought. *Strong. Fierce.*

Sara went quickly to get her few possessions. Her eyes filled with tears as she realized that this could very well be the last time she ever saw her family again. Looking around the rooms where she had known so much happiness brought a lump to her throat. *Please God*, she thought, *take care of them.*

Antonius spoke to her father for several minutes before he mounted his horse again. Had he told her father what was to become of Dathan? When Sara returned to his side, her bundle of clothes under her arm, Antonius reached down and lifted her to the saddle in front of him. A familiar feeling washed over Sara as he wrapped his arms around her and lifted the reins. Touching his feet to the horse's sides, they leapt forward. When Sara looked back, she saw her father and mother in each other's arms. Her father looked frail with his grief. Sara had never seen him that way before, and she felt his pain as her own. Turning around, she kept her eyes forward.

They rode in silence some time before Sara finally dared a question. "Tribune?"

She regretted questioning him when he leaned forward to hear her, his cheek brushing against hers. Her heart jumped and her breathing became shallow.

"Yes?"

Swallowing her fear, her voice came out hesitantly. "My brother, Dathan. Must he be sent to the galleys?"

Antonius leaned back and looked down at the girl in front of him. All he could see was the brown silk of her tresses hanging long and straight in front of him. He was almost tempted to run the strands through his fingers. Bringing his thoughts up short, he tried to answer her question without hurting her. He had remembered where he had seen Dathan before, after he left her home. In Ephesus, at the legionnaires' headquarters. Gambling with the soldiers.

"Your brother has a lesson to learn," he told her calmly. "I have seen your brother when he gambles."

Sara jerked her head around in surprise. Antonius stared down into her large brown eyes for several seconds. "Oh yes, Sara." The huskiness of his voice caused a fluttering in the pit of her stomach. "He has the sickness. When he gambles nothing else matters. Not you. Not your family. Not anything."

"But he's only a boy," she told him softly.

She watched as his eyes dilated to black obsidian. He snorted and Sara turned away, unable to withstand the scorn she saw in his face.

"When I was his age I had already joined the Roman legion and saw my first battle."

Orion shifted beneath him, and Antonius took a moment to adjust his position, pulling Sara more securely against him.

"Because of Dathan your family have lost everything and are slaves of a Roman. You are here with me now not knowing what I have planned for you." Antonius could feel her breathing deepen and almost laughed aloud. "I would have died before I let such shame come upon my family."

"Perhaps so," Sara agreed. "But I fail to see how the galleys will accomplish anything. It can't change what has already transpired." There were tears in her voice, though she held her body rigidly erect, and he could not see her face.

"Some of my soldiers have had the same sickness," he told her roughly, not unmoved by the tears. "The only cure for them is to get them as far away from the temptation as possible. There will be no time to think of such foolishness where your brother is going, and maybe it will help him to realize just what he has lost."

Sara thought of her brother in the bowels of a ship day in and day out, never seeing the sun. Every day, rowing, rowing. Chained to others doing the same. Her heart cried out with the pain and tears flowed freely down her cheeks. Poor Dathan. So full of life. So impetuous. What would become of him? For that matter what would become of her?

She could see Ephesus laid out before her as they slowly approached the city. She had only been here twice with her family, even though they lived close. Instead of excitement as she had felt before, she felt only dread. Somewhere down there among the ports her brother was being chained in a hold. Somewhere down there was her future, but the only future she could see was filled with sorrow. Without realizing it, she leaned her head back against Antonius' chest.

The sudden warmth of Sara's body against his brought Antonius' thoughts sharply back to the present. It suddenly came to Antonius just what she must be going through. The fear she must be feeling. The thought of someone doing something so barbarous to Diana almost made his blood boil. He felt a moment's guilt until he realized that he had done all of this for Diana. Pulling Sara tighter against him, he tried to let her know that she was safe. He had snatched her from her home and family, sent her brother to the galleys, purchased her home through less than ethical circumstances, and yet through it all she had maintained her composure. She certainly had no reason to trust him. Suddenly, he felt very protective.

"You have nothing to be afraid of, Sara," he whispered in her ear and felt her shiver. Mistaking the response, he pressed his lips tightly together. He decided he needed to give her time. He remembered the time he had spent in her company. For the past several weeks his thoughts had returned to her from time to time, wishing at times that he could be in her presence. Just being around her had brought peace to his troubled soul, if only momentarily. When Diana's condition had worsened, he had remembered the healer who had treated Sara. Although he had some of the finest physicians in Rome attending to Diana, they had been able to do nothing. Desperate, Antonius had decided to seek the healer out. Instead he had come away with Sara. In time she would see what he needed her for, and maybe, just maybe, she could help Diana. Firmly he pushed the guilt feelings aside and tried not to think too much about the future.

four

Antonius led his horse through the back streets of Ephesus, bypassing any would-be gossips. He went through large wooden gates set inside six-foot-high concrete walls that surrounded his outer garden. A servant was waiting when he stopped his mount, taking the reins from Antonius, who had to smile. Only Gallus could handle the huge stallion and him no more than a boy of fourteen. They had forged a bond between them precipitated by the boy's love of anything equine.

Sliding from the saddle, Antonius reached up, placing his hands around Sara's tiny waist and helping her to dismount. He patted Orion before releasing him to the boy's custody. "Be sure he is fed, watered and brushed down." Antonius knew he didn't need to remind the boy, but it was part of a long-standing game the two played. As usual, the boy's lips pushed out in a pout and he told the horse, "One day I will take you away from such a mean master."

Sara's eyes widened in shock. She glanced at Antonius only to find him grinning at the boy. Realizing that this interplay between the two was not serious, she smiled slightly. It was good to know that Antonius had a sense of humor and treated his slaves like people instead of dogs.

Glancing around her, Sara was awed by the large villa. Huge Doric columns rose majestically upwards ending at a roof line that gave the front entrance a spatial elegance. Antonius led her through the open door into the atrium where the bright light of the afternoon sun shone through the opening in the ceiling. Brightly colored wall paintings and cold marble floor tiles decorated the room. Sara had never experienced such wealth in her life, even though among the Jews her father was considered a wealthy man.

Antonius watched her silently, knowing that whatever the circumstances, she would find a way to adjust. "Come, Sara," he told her. "I will show you around while I explain certain things to you."

She regarded him soberly. "About your sister?"

He nodded. "That and other things."

They went through a large doorway supported by Composite columns into the peristyle. A fountain tinkled in the center of the courtyard, surrounded by trees, shrubs and flowers. The color and beauty almost took Sara's breath away. Sunlight spilled through a large opening in the ceiling. Leading her to a bench near the fountain, Antonius motioned for her to sit.

"Anyone who resides at this house is welcome to use the peristyle, but only if the area is not being utilized for some reason." He motioned towards the other end of the courtyard, and Sara could see another garden through another opening.

"That is the fruit and vegetable garden. You are allowed there anytime."

Sara understood. With each word he uttered she felt more and more the shackles of bondage. He made very clear the differences between them.

Sitting down next to her, Antonius picked a flower and began to slowly pull it apart. "My sister is dying," he told her, and Sara could hear the pain in his voice. "The doctors say there is nothing more that can be done." He sighed in frustration. He looked at Sara before he turned his attention back to the flower, dropping a petal on the ground. "They're not even sure what ails her."

Sara's eyes clouded with sympathy. "I'm sorry."

Antonius turned to her and smiled wryly. "Are you? After all that I've done? Why should you care about a Roman?"

Taking her time before answering, Sarah looked up at the sky through the opening in the ceiling and stared pensively at the feathery clouds drifting above them. Oh, to be on the hillsides watching the sheep graze, their soft bleating echoing across the knolls.

"It is true that I have no love for the Romans," she told him softly. "But neither do I hate them."

Antonius watched her, his eyes sliding from the straight dark hair across skin bronzed by the sun, to the sandals on her feet. His gaze returned to her face and rested there. She had a flawless complexion and shimmering brown eyes that seemed to see into his soul. She could not be called beautiful, even by her own countrymen's standards. Still, there was something that caused a person to want to be close to her. A gentleness. A peacefulness that seemed to come from within.

He noticed again the sheen of her dark skin. No Roman woman would be caught dead with skin of such a color. It seemed too plebeian. Roman women took pains to make sure that their skin was creamy and white. Antonius found the contrast rather stimulating. Shaking his head, he turned away.

"Come. I will introduce you to my sister."

Standing, he helped Sara to her feet, which she found rather disconcerting. He held her hand a moment longer than necessary, though Sara could tell it was without conscious thought. Letting go of her hand, he brushed a hand through his dark hair, breathing out a long sigh.

"Sara, I need to explain something to you. I brought you here not only to be a servant—I already have more than I can use—but to be a friend. A companion for my sister." He stared into her eyes, willing her to understand. "She's very lonely. It's harder for her than most because for so long she was the toast of Ephesus, even at her age. She had many friends and plenty of them men. Now, no one comes to see her, except perhaps my friend Flavius."

He could tell by her puzzled expression that she didn't understand what he was trying to say. He tried again. "People in Ephesus are concerned with their health. We have an abundance of physicians to attend to their needs, but they have a tendency to fear what they cannot understand."

Sara looked up suddenly, catching the intent look of Antonius' eyes. Hers were filled with comprehension. "Is your sister's illness contagious?"

"No."

"You know that for certain?"

"Yes," he told her adamantly. "No one else in this house has been ill, nor I for that matter, and Diana has been ill for some time. Ever since. . ."

He stopped suddenly and Sara wondered what he had been about to say.

"Come. I will introduce you, then we will talk again."

Sara followed him up the staircase that led to a balcony above. He stopped outside a door and tapped gently.

"Come." The voice was muted, but sadness laced the one word.

Antonius opened the door and went inside, Sara close on his heels. The room was darkened against the afternoon sun. A figure reclined on the bed, but it was too dark to tell much about it. Sara assumed that it was Diana.

"Antonius!"

A thrill ran through Sara at the intensity of the greeting. Happiness, longing, and desperation all rolled into one. It was obvious that Antonius was Diana's whole existence.

Diana buried her face in her hands and started weeping softly. "Oh Antonius! Where have you been? I called and called, but Decimus said you had gone."

Antonius went to her and gathered her gently into his arms. Diana clung to him as he tried to soothe her distress. Sara felt a lump in her own throat. What must Diana's life be like that a visit from her own brother was what she longed for with every fiber of her being.

"Come now, little dove," he remonstrated softly. "You'll make yourself ill. Dry your eyes and see what I have brought for you."

The sobbing stopped instantly, but Sara could see the sheen in the eyes lifted to Antonius' face.

"What have you brought me?"

The childlike cadences of the voice were all the more surprising when a servant came in and pulled back the drapes from the window, and Sara could see the figure in the bed for the first time. Blonde hair, the color of the sun in the afternoon, was matted around a porcelain white face that had to be at least as old as Sara. Blue eyes that were almost violet turned to regard Sara.

Antonius motioned Sara into the room. "I have brought you a companion." At Diana's startled look, he continued. "Now you need never be alone again."

Sara felt her heart sink. Was she to be the slave of a lonely, ill girl who had nothing to live for, it would seem, except her brother? Sara felt compassion for the girl, but wondered if she too would be required to stay in a dark bedroom all day. Flicking her eyes around the room, Sara was conscious of marble tables, chests carved from cedar and silk draperies which bespoke of wealth and luxury. A gilded prison, but a prison nevertheless. She chastised herself for her selfishness. What would Jesus have her do? With the question came peace. She would do whatever she could to make Diana's days happier.

Diana opened her mouth to say something, but stopped. She turned to Sara, and a sudden smile lit up her features. Sara felt a twinge of envy. With her hair combed and dressed properly, Diana would be remarkably beautiful. Diana's eyes took on an animation of their own.

"Hello." Her voice had brightened considerably. Sara searched her eyes and found only warm friendliness. She returned the girl's smile and felt something pass between them.

"I know we will be friends," Diana told her, and Sara believed her, relaxing visibly.

Antonius watched the exchange with satisfaction. He had done the right thing. He knew it now, though he felt a slight pang when he remembered Abigail's face as he had ridden away with her daughter. Arrogance quickly resurfaced. What did it matter? They were only Jews, while he as a Roman soldier had a job to do. He had been on the brink of a decision that would have altered his life completely. Now he felt like he could postpone what he considered to be the inevitable. Someday he would have to resign his commission in the legion to stay home and be with Diana. How much longer she had he didn't know, and his heart sank when he thought of life without her. Every time he had been sent away, when he returned he found Diana much worse than when he had left. It would take weeks to get her back to normal. At least as normal as possible in her circumstances.

Releasing Diana from his arms, Antonius rose from the bed. "I will leave you two to get to know each other. I have some things that need my attention."

Diana clung to his hand, staring imploringly up into his face.

"It's all right," he told her quietly. "I will be in the office. I have to go over the shipping lists with Abijah. I will be close by if you need me."

Reluctantly, Diana released his hand. When Antonius reached the door, he turned back to Sara. "I will speak to you later, after Diana is settled for the night."

Sara nodded, swallowing hard when the door closed behind him. She turned to Diana, who was watching her curiously.

"You are not Roman. Nor Greek for that matter."

"No," Sara explained. "I am Jewish."

"Ah. A slave?" she questioned.

Sara hesitated. "I suppose you could say so."

Diana quirked an eyebrow, and looked remarkably like her brother. "You're not sure?"

Again Sara hesitated. "I consider no man my master."

Diana's eyebrows flew upwards, her mouth quirking with humor. "It's obvious you've never had a lover."

Color suffused Sara's face. Thinking carefully before answering, she finally told Diana, "No. That is true. But that is not what I meant. Actually, what I meant to say is that I already have a master."

"Of course you do, silly. Antonius."

"No." Sara was being drawn into a conversation she didn't think she was ready for. Somehow, this did not seem the right time. "I serve my God."

"Oh!" Diana relaxed. "Is that all. Which one?"

"To the Jews, there is only one."

Diana wrinkled her nose. "Sounds boring to me. But it doesn't really matter. I no longer believe in deities anyway. I have asked healing from them all, paid a large sum of money, even, and still nothing." She settled herself back on the bed, her face filled with despair. "You may serve your God, Sara. I suppose it doesn't hurt to have faith in something." The desolation in her voice convinced Sara that there was nothing left for Diana to believe in. In time, perhaps Sara could share with her God's love. Even the Apostle Paul had shared the good news with the Romans. Could she do any less?

"My lady," Sara asked hesitantly. "Would you like me to dress your hair?"

Diana turned her head lethargically on the pillow. "What for? There's no one to see me."

Sudden inspiration made Sara pause. "There's Tribune Antonius."

Diana thought about it. She supposed that with everything Antonius did for her, the least she could do was look presentable. It had been a long while since she had cared anything about her looks. Antonius would love her anyway, but still some measure of pride returned to her.

"Yes, Sara. That would be good. Have Decimus bring some water."

Sara smiled. "Yes, my lady." When Sara opened the door, she found a young man waiting outside. He quickly got to his feet. Although he was young, his handsome features bespoke of early manhood. His short white tunic showed to perfection his strong muscular body. Blonde hair shimmered in the afternoon sun and his clear blue eyes regarded her expectantly. Sara assumed that he was required to stay there in case Diana needed anything.

"You wish for something?" he asked quickly.

"I need water to wash my lady's hair." The boy's eyes lit up, and it was clear to Sara that Diana was liked by the boy. "Can you find me some fragrance for the rinse water, and some olive oil?"

"Right away, my lady." He turned and hurried away.

Sara went back into the room. "Where are the brushes, my lady?"

Diana frowned at her. "You needn't call me my lady. I don't want you to seem just another servant. I want us to be friends. Call me Diana."

Refusing to consider what the Tribune might think of such an arrangement, Sara nodded. Diana motioned to the dressing table. "You'll find the brushes and things over there."

A tap at the door signaled the return of Decimus with the water. He went to the corner and set the urn next to a small marble tub. Going to the door, he turned. "If there is anything else, I am right outside." He closed the door quietly behind him.

Sara went to Diana and helped her to sit up in bed. Taking the brush, Sara began to gently stroke Diana's hair, starting at the bottom and working her way up. Eventually her hair was free of tangles. Although Diana's hair was long, it was thin and dull, an obvious sign of ill health. Sara had done her best to make sure she didn't hurt the girl, knowing that her head would be sensitive after such a long period without care. Since Sara found no evidence of lice, she assumed that someone had washed Diana's hair before, or maybe her sickness hadn't been that long.

Pulling a chair carved from Lebanon cedar over to the marble tub, Sara prepared to wash Diana's hair. She kept up a constant flow of chatter that required little effort on Diana's part, but helped her to relax.

Sara helped Diana to the seat and began to gently wash her hair. She rinsed it with clear water that turned a dirty brown as it flowed through Diana's hair. Deciding to wash it several times, Sara had to first ask Decimus to bring more water.

When the rinse water finally ran clear, Sara took a towel and began to pat the hair dry. She poured a measure of oil from the cruse and began to massage it into Diana's scalp. As she worked her fingers through Diana's hair, she began to hum a tune that her mother had sung to her as a child. The soothing melody helped Diana relax and soon she closed her eyes.

"That feels wonderful, Sara. I don't know why I never bothered before."

Taking the brush, Sara first washed it in some water before using it to brush out Diana's hair again. Finally, her golden tresses lay curling against her back, the olive oil giving it extra shine.

"Would you like to change outfits, my. . .Diana? This one is a little wet."

Submitting patiently to Sara's ministrations, it wasn't long before Diana was settled back against the pillows on her sleeping couch. Sara decided that enough had been done for one day. Diana was tired, but already she looked like a changed girl. A feeling of accomplishment engulfed Sara. Given time, Sara knew she could come to love this unhappy Roman girl.

The soft regular breathing told Sara that Diana was asleep. Taking Diana's soiled tunic, she went to the window and pulled the drapes to a little. Enough to keep out most of the light, but not enough to give it the tomblike appearance it had before.

Opening the door, she found Decimus waiting expectantly.

"Could you empty the water?" she asked him and he nodded his head, going past her and into the room. Picking up the tub, he started to pass Sara, his eyes quickly surveying the sleeping figure. A smile crossed his lips fleetingly.

"What do I do with the soiled tunic?" she asked.

He turned his look full upon Sara. "Just leave it by the door on the balcony. I will see to it. The master wanted to see you when his sister fell asleep." His eyes went back to the bed. "She doesn't stay awake very long at a time. She's very weak. What you've accomplished today is a miracle."

Following him back down the stone balustrade, Sara wondered if perhaps he might be right. Had her Lord sent her here for a purpose? Like Paul who was in chains himself and still managed to win most of the household of Caesar to the Lord? The thought was disturbing. And what of the Tribune? What part did he have to play in all of this drama? The house seemed suddenly sinister. There was much of the Evil One at work here, but praying to the Lord helped to push back the darkness. For the time being, she would be a light in this house. She would try not to be afraid, and she would try her best to show The Way to these infidels. Already she was beginning to love one. She prayed fervently that she would not love the other.

five

Sara entered the bibliotheca behind Decimus. She stared around her at the large number of papyrus scrolls that rested in cubicles in the walls. Manuscripts seemed to be on every available surface. Sara had heard of such libraries before, but had never seen one.

Antonius was leaning over a table when they entered. He straightened up and motioned Sara forward. His eyes were questioning, so Sara answered him. "Diana is asleep."

He nodded. "And? What did you think?"

"She seems very fragile and lonely. Other than that I know very little."

Decimus interrupted. "My lady allowed her to wash her hair. And she changed her tunic, also."

Antonius looked at Sara in surprise. "How did you manage this?"

Sara shrugged. "I merely suggested it."

"I have suggested this also, but she has never done it for me," Antonius told her.

"Perhaps you didn't have the right incentive," Sara told him mysteriously.

"And that is?"

Even Decimus seemed intrigued, waiting for her to answer.

"I only suggested that she might wish to look nice for you, Tribune."

Antonius felt humbled by Diana's love, but he was also filled with exhilaration. Sara had managed to do in a few hours what he and the other servants hadn't been able to do in months. Fortune had smiled upon him when She led him to Sara that day. He would have to arrange a sacrifice to the gods. Perhaps Fortuna, goddess of luck.

He turned to Decimus. "From now on, when Sara is with Diana, you no longer need to wait outside her door. But when Sara needs something, be prepared for her call."

"Yes, my lord."

Decimus and Antonius exchanged glances, smiling at each other before the boy left the room. Sara watched him depart.

"Decimus, is he a slave also?"

Antonius felt uncomfortable. "Yes." The short, clipped word told Sara that he would say nothing more on the subject. If Sara wanted to know anything more about Decimus, she would have to find out from Decimus himself.

Rolling up the papyrus he had been examining, Antonius used it as an excuse to turn away from Sara's accusing eyes. Her censure bothered him, but she asked him a different question from what he was expecting.

"When did Diana become sick? Was she visiting out of the country?"

Antonius shook his head. "No."

He seemed disinclined to speak further, so Sara pressed harder. "It would help me, Tribune, to know how to deal with her sickness. What do the doctors say?"

He waited so long to answer that Sara thought he wasn't going to. Finally, he looked at her angrily. "They say she is under some kind of curse from the gods."

"That's it? That's all they say?"

Antonius nodded his head. Putting away the last scroll, he motioned to the doorway. "Let's go into the atrium where it's cooler and I will try to explain things."

Sara followed him through the doorway and into the atrium. For the first time, she noticed the scenes depicted on the wall hangings. Various gods played among the earth and the heavens, while people gave offerings. Other scenes depicted the battles of the Roman army. Sara shivered with distaste. Noticing her response, Antonius hid a smile.

"Perhaps the peristyle would be better."

Sara followed him through the marble portals to the seat beside the fountain. He motioned for her to be seated, but he stood before her trying to gather his thoughts.

"Almost a year ago, my sister was engaged to a Roman noble. They were very much in love, but shortly after their engagement party he was killed when a horse threw him. He was a friend of mine, also." He stopped and Sara watched his eyes glaze over at the remembered pain. "For a time, Diana refused to see anyone. Even me. She hid in her bedroom and would scream if anyone so much as tried to come near her. I called for the physicians, but they needed to examine her to see if there was anything more than grief wrong with her." Slowly he sank to the bench beside her, a faraway look in his eyes.

"And was there?" She questioned, even though she thought she already knew the answer.

He glanced at her uncomprehendingly. "What? Oh. . .not that they could find. One physician left a draught for her to take to help her sleep. It was the first sleep she had had in almost a week." He leaned his head into his hands. "I thought her mind was gone. I have seen this happen before when someone lost a loved one."

Sara was becoming suspicious. "And did she take the sleeping draught again?"

Antonius glanced at her impatiently. "Only when she couldn't sleep. What are you trying to say?"

"I'm not trying to say anything. I was just wondering."

"Well, you can ask questions of the physician when he comes tomorrow," Antonius told her. "He comes once a week to care for her."

Sara decided to try again. "And how is she after the physician leaves?"

He took a moment to think about it. "Quiet, I suppose you could say. Very lethargic. But she sleeps better."

"She is sleeping well now," Sara reasoned, and he looked at her in wonder.

"That's true, but then she sleeps a lot anyway."

"Then why should she need a sleeping draught?" she demanded softly.

Antonius jumped to his feet. "Look Sara, I don't have all the answers. I just have to trust the physicians to do the best for her. Let's not speak of this anymore tonight." He lifted Sara to her feet. "Let's go and check on Diana and then you can have something to eat. You must be starved."

Again Sara marveled that he would care so much for a mere slave. She walked up the concrete stairs with him to the balcony that surrounded the peristyle. He went to Diana's door and knocked softly. When there was no answer, he quietly pushed open the door and peeked inside. Sara followed him into the room and had to smile at Diana's figure curled up asleep. Antonius laid a hand against her cheek and sighed with relief.

"There's no fever. Sometimes she has bouts with fever and nausea. But not tonight."

Antonius picked up the tray of food beside the bed that was for the most part untouched. Sara wrinkled her nose at the disgusting blend of greasy foods.

"Tribune, is that the kind of food she always eats?"

Frowning, Antonius studied the tray. "Is there something wrong with the food, too?" he asked sarcastically. "Tell me, are you a Jewish healer as well as the old man?"

Sara shook her head. "Ahaz has taught our people much about different healing balms and herbs, but he is the master. It doesn't take a healer to realize that greasy food might be indigestible to a sick stomach."

Antonius seemed to ponder what she said. Shrugging his

shoulders, he told her in exasperation, "The physicians said she needed the fat."

"I see."

Two little words with a wealth of condemnation. Antonius whirled on his feet and left the room. When he reached the balcony, he told Sara, "Go and get something to eat and then return to Diana. Sometimes she wakes during the night and is frightened."

Gritting her teeth at his arrogant tone, she followed him down the stairs. "The kitchen is through there," he told her coldly, and Sara wondered what had made him so angry. There was no way that she could know that her questions had made him feel remiss in his duty to his sister. He decided that tomorrow he would ask more questions of the physicians.

Sara ate a solitary meal of dates and oranges. She had very little appetite and the emotional turmoil of the day was beginning to catch up with her. When she returned to Diana's room, she found that Decimus had placed a sleeping couch in the room for her. Sara smiled slightly at his thoughtfulness. He couldn't know that all of her life she had slept on a mat on the floor.

She went to the water urn in the corner and freshened herself before going to the couch and throwing herself on her knees. She leaned against the bed, her heart nearly breaking with her grief. Prayers went swiftly up on behalf of her parents and Dathan, and she asked God to take care of them. She prayed for Diana, that God would heal her body and her soul. She prayed that Antonius would be a kind master. Lastly, she prayed for herself. Peace settled down around her, soothing, and she knew that God was with her. That's how Decimus found her the next morning, still on her knees.

❧

Sara could hear voices coming from the peristyle, so she

hastily turned her steps away and headed instead for the kitchen. She had made friends with Bacchus, the kitchen cook. He was kind, but could become very angry if someone so much as hinted that there was something wrong with his food.

"Bacchus, what kind of food would you fix for someone who was very ill if you had the choice?" Sara asked him.

"Humph. No one has asked me, but if they did I would tell them that soups and broths and fresh fruit would be the best thing."

Sara nodded. "I knew you were a wise man."

Bacchus puffed up at the praise. This little Jewish slave was intelligent for a woman. Already in the week she had been here she had made some subtle changes. Changes he heartily approved of.

Decimus entered the kitchen. "Sara, the master wishes your presence in the peristyle."

Heart thumping fearfully, Sara went quickly, only to find Antonius with another man. She hesitated in the doorway, but Antonius motioned her to come in.

"Sara, you probably don't remember my friend Flavius, but he was with me the day I shot you with the arrow."

Flavius stared at the girl curiously. She looked nothing like the little girl they had found on the hillside. He couldn't know that Antonius had ordered her to wear more colorful clothes, refusing to let her wear the brown she favored that made her look so colorless. Indeed, Flavius found her rather attractive, in a strange sort of way.

"I have told Flavius about the change you have wrought in Diana, and he thought maybe Diana might be inclined to see him," Antonius told her. "Go and find out if Diana will have a visitor?"

"In her bedchamber?" Sara blurted. Color flamed into her face when Antonius smiled mockingly and Flavius burst out laughing. Turning, she fled up the stairs and entered Diana's room, slamming the door behind her. These Romans had no shame whatsoever. Was nothing sacred to them?

Diana was sitting up in bed, her hair curled becomingly around her slender shoulders. Although Sara had managed to make some change in her appearance, Diana was still lethargic and had very little energy to do much of anything. Sara was beginning to form some opinions of her own, having watched proceedings for the last week.

She still shivered when she thought of the day the physician had come. He had given Decimus the sleeping powders that Diana used almost every night. Sara was horrified when he pulled a container from his bag and took out little insects. Making an incision on Diana's arm with a small knife, he placed the insects on the cut where they greedily fed off Diana's blood. As each insect became gorged, he removed it and put another in its place. Covering her mouth, Sara ran from the room.

When she returned, Diana lay pale and listless against the covers. Going to her side, Sara took Diana's hand into her own, gently stroking her palm and wrist. Diana smiled slightly.

"Not used to a little blood, Sara? Don't worry, you soon will be."

Sara refrained from comment. There was no way she could ever become used to such a gruesome sight. And if there was any way possible, she intended to prevent it from happening again.

That had been almost a week ago, and Diana seemed better today. But the physician would come again tomorrow, and then it would start all over again.

"My lady, there is someone here who would like to see you."

Diana's face registered her surprise. "Who would want to

see me?" she asked sarcastically. "No one has cared enough before."

"Perhaps they would have if they thought you wanted it," Sara answered.

"I don't wish to see anyone. Except Antonius." Sara turned to leave the room so she could deliver the message, but before she reached the door Diana stopped her.

"Wait! Who is it?"

"His name is Tribune Flavius, my lady," Sara told her and watched her eyes spark with interest.

"Flavius? Here?" Her face took on a faraway expression and she smiled slightly. She quirked an eyebrow at Sara. "He was in love with me at one time, you know. Before. . ."

Watching the frown forming on her face, Sara hurried to turn her thoughts. "So, do you wish to see him?" Diana hesitated so long Sara decided she must not have heard. About to repeat the question, Diana suddenly turned wistful eyes to her.

"I would like to change first." Sara smiled with pleasure and hurried to the chest that held Diana's colorful array of tunics.

"Let me have the royal blue tunic and the soft blue palla," Diana suggested. "At least they will not make me look so ill."

Sara helped her replace her tunic and then wrapped the palla around Diana's shoulders and waist.

"Would you like me to braid your hair?" Sara asked her.

Excitement began to sparkle in Diana's eyes. Sara rarely saw that look. Only when Antonius came to visit.

"Yes, braid my hair. There are some pearls on my dressing table that you can use also."

When Sara returned to the garden she found Flavius waiting expectantly.

"She will see you now, Tribune."

His brown eyes ignited with joy in response, and Sara thought that he was a most handsome man. She smiled softly at him and then turned her eyes to Antonius. He was thunderstruck. Sara had to stifle a grin.

Antonius turned to Sara, his mouth open in surprise. "What magic did you use to accomplish this?"

Sara frowned at him. "Not magic," she stressed, "just love and encouragement."

Both Flavius and Antonius regarded her somberly. Antonius knew that what she said was true, for he had noticed a bond forming between his sister and Sara. It was hard to imagine, but they truly seemed to love each other. Like sisters. Sara could get Diana to do things that even Antonius couldn't manage. Antonius felt a twinge of jealousy.

"I'll come with you, Flavius," he told the young man.

Sara followed both men up the stairs. They paused outside Diana's chamber, but Sara motioned them inside. The drapes were opened wide to receive the full morning sun, which gave a glow to Diana's blonde hair. Although it was still thin from her illness, it glowed with the care Sara had been giving it.

Diana looked pale, but beautiful. Flavius couldn't take his eyes from her and Antonius stared with awe at the transformation. He glanced at Sara, who was staring with pride at Diana.

Flavius went forward, taking Diana's hand into his and raising it to his lips. "You look truly beautiful. Worthy of Aphrodite herself," he told her softly.

Diana blushed at the compliment and the color made her look healthier, adding a touch of innocent beauty to her face. "Flavius," she murmured. "I have missed you."

Sara could see him swallow hard, his eyes roving restlessly over Diana's face. "If that is so, lovely one, but say the word and I will be by your side every day."

Diana gave a trill of laughter. "And what would Caesar have to say about that? Far be it from me to cause one of his most loyal officers to desert."

Antonius stepped forward. "Diana, it is good to see you looking so well." He could see the dark circles under her eyes, the translucency of her skin, but there was life in her eyes. He began to have hope. How much of this was due to Sara who tended her constantly?

"If you don't mind, I have some things I need to discuss with Sara," Antonius informed them. Placing a hand on Flavius' shoulder, he gave it a squeeze. "I will see you later."

Flavius barely noticed their departure, and Antonius grinned at Sara. She preceded him out the door, but left it open behind her. Antonius' mouth quirked slightly and he shook his head slightly. The girl was a definite innocent.

Sara followed Antonius through the atrium, her eyes averted from the wall hangings she so despised. He took her through to the triclinium, an adjoining room that was sometimes used when they entertained guests for a meal. It had been a long time since this room had been occupied, but Antonius knew it would be less offensive to Sara's decided ideas of purity. He motioned her to be seated on a small chaise, and he sat down next to her.

"Sara, I don't know how you have managed to wrought such a transformation in my sister in such a short time, but I want you to know that I am truly thankful." He hesitated, his eyes searching hers. Sara waited patiently for him to continue. Something was bothering him, and eventually he would tell her what it was. She began to feel a little apprehensive, but he finally continued. "I want to repay you in some way."

That she was amazed was an understatement. She searched his face for some clue to where this conversation was leading, but could find none.

"I am a slave, Tribune. I expect no payment," she told him softly.

He waved his hand in dismissal of her statement, frowning in annoyance. "Neither Diana nor I see you as such."

Sara was confused, cocking her head slightly. "Then how do you see me, sir?"

He watched her so long that Sara thought he wasn't going to answer. "I didn't bring you here to discuss how I see you. I brought you here to tell you that tomorrow I will take you home to visit your parents."

Sara's face filled with delight, and forgetting herself, she threw herself into Antonius' arms, hugging him joyously. When she would have pulled away, Antonius held her more firmly. He grinned at her as her face suffused with color.

"Perhaps I should take you to see your parents more often," he teased.

"Please, Tribune," she begged, struggling for release. Antonius bent and kissed her nose before quickly releasing her. In an instant, his demeanor changed from playful to serious.

"We have to assure Diana that we won't be gone long. I don't want everything undone that has already been accomplished. If this can't be done, then we cannot go."

Sara's heart sank. Although Diana seemed slightly better, she still had boughts of depression and would burst into tears at the least little provocation. Sara was afraid to even ask. Fortunately, the way was made clear when she and Antonius returned to Diana's room and found Flavius on the verge of departure.

"She's very tired," he told Antonius. "She needs to rest now."

Antonius could see Diana's eyes starting to glaze with fatigue, but still she tried to maintain a facade.

"Don't forget, Flavius," she told him in a coquettish voice.

"You promised to spend time with me tomorrow."

Flavius smiled, taking her hand to his lips again. "I will be here even if I have to take on Caesar himself," he told her teasingly.

After the two men left, Diana quickly began to droop. Sara rushed to her and helped her ready herself for sleep. Sara would wait until later to discuss her and Antonius' trip to see her parents. She begged God to let nothing happen to hinder them. The only problem she was having was the thought of being alone with Antonius again. Remembering the feel of his arms around her, she buried her face in her hands. "Please God," she begged, "Don't let this happen to me."

six

Sara felt the exhilaration of riding in a chariot for the first time. Antonius had chosen this means of transportation because Sara didn't know how to ride a horse. And although it may have given him some pleasure to have her in his arms again, he didn't think it would be pleasurable for Sara.

It had been easier than either Sara or Antonius had believed to leave the villa, partly, they were certain, because of Flavius. Diana had been more animated than Antonius had seen her in a long time. Perhaps Sara was right and Diana was beginning to heal, if not physically, then at least mentally. Antonius had assured her that they would return before the physician's visit that afternoon.

Sara pressed herself closer to the front of the chariot, trying to ease herself away from Antonius' form. He smiled slightly, recognizing the maneuver. His pride was somewhat affected since he had never had a woman turn away from him before. He decided to tease her a little. Using a flock of cranes as an excuse, he leaned forward and pointed them out to Sara. He felt her body stiffen as his chest pressed against her back. Antonius grinned. She had nowhere else to go.

"Tell me, Sara," he whispered in her ear. "Did you leave someone behind when I took you away?"

Choosing to misunderstand him, she snapped in irritation, "Of course I did. Isn't that who we're going to see?"

He ignored her displeasure. "I mean a man. Did you not have someone you were attached to?" he asked her softly, his breath brushing against her ear. He felt her shiver and grinned again.

"I had no one," she told him stonily.

Antonius decided to relieve her of her misery and pulled back, adjusting the reins in his hands. The beauty of the day filled him with vitality and taking a deep breath, he lifted his eyes heavenward, giving thanks to the gods. As though she could read his thoughts, Sara spoke with the same exhilaration.

"God has truly smiled upon the earth today."

"Your God?"

Sara pressed her lips together. "I have told you. There is only one God."

"That is your belief. We Romans believe a person should be allowed to choose whichever god they desire."

"How kind," Sara told him, her voice dripping with sarcasm.

Antonius frowned. Although he had meant what he told Sara about not seeing her as a slave, he still felt aggravated by her lack of respect.

"Why should anyone believe in your God over the others?" he asked her.

"Tell me, Tribune. How do you picture a god? Is he not all powerful?" she queried.

"Of course."

"How is it then that your Roman gods can be destroyed by one another? Punished by one another for their misdeeds?"

Antonius chose to answer her question with one of his own. "And your God cannot be destroyed?"

"No," she told him seriously. "He has been since before time, and will continue after time ceases to be."

He tried to puzzle out what she was saying. "And you believe only one God could create the whole earth? And everything in it?"

"One time," she told him, "I went to a wedding banquet. Several of the women—aunts, sisters, cousins, mothers

—were trying to prepare the feast. Each had their own idea of how it should be done. It was total chaos."

Antonius smiled wryly. "I have seen this also. I get what you are trying to say. If more than one being tried to create the same thing, we would have the same result."

"Your gods are capricious," she reiterated. "My God is unchanging. His word is His oath, and nothing can cause Him to break His word. He is a loving God who cares for His people."

"And if your God cares for you so much, then why are you a slave?" he asked her derisively.

Sara had no answer. She had asked herself the same question over and over, but she had faith that God had put her where she was for a purpose.

"No answer, Sara?"

"No one knows the mind of God, Tribune. If we did, He wouldn't be God."

For the rest of the journey, Antonius thought about what she had said. As they neared her village, he could feel the rising excitement emanating from her. He followed the path he remembered, turning away from the spot where he had first encountered Sara that fateful day. Unerringly, he made his way to Sara's front door. Both the front door and the shop door were closed against the increasing heat from the sun.

Things seemed too quiet, and when Sara would have jumped down, he held her back. His soldier's instinct told him something was seriously wrong.

"Stay put," he commanded.

"But. . ."

"Do as I say, Sara. If you get out of this chariot, I'll have you flogged."

Sara paled at the threat, swallowing down her anger and impatience. Antonius got out of the chariot and cautiously approached the house. He knocked on the door, waiting for a response. None came. Sara was frightened. She, too, could sense that something was amiss.

Antonius applied his shoulder to the door and it creaked open on its leather hinges. He peered into the gloom.

"Sara. Come here."

She was at his side in an instant. He nodded his head towards the corner and she could see a figure laying on a mat. Pushing the door open wider to let in the light, Sara could make out the figure of her mother, her eyes closed.

"Mother?" Sara's voice echoed eerily around the room. Quickly she went to Abigail and laid a hand against her forehead. Bending closer, she was startled when her mother suddenly opened her eyes.

"Sara?"

Sara could barely understand her, her voice was so faint. "Yes, Mother. It's me. What has happened to you? Where is Father?"

Instead of answering, Abigail closed her eyes again. Sara looked at Antonius in alarm. "My mother is ill."

Sensing a presence, Antonius whirled quickly to face the door. Jubal stood in the opening, his eyes on Sara. He was thinner than when she had left a week ago, and he looked like an old man. His shoulders were bent as though he were carrying the weight of the whole world on his shoulders.

"Sara? You have come home."

His tired voice was the last straw for Sara. She threw herself into her father's arms and burst into tears. "What has happened here? What's wrong with Mother? What's wrong with you?"

Although his strength had been diminished, Sara felt as though he would surely crush her ribs.

"My baby," he whispered over and over.

Antonius was stricken with remorse. Had he been responsible for all of this? When he remembered the strength of the old Jew, his regal bearing, and then saw the way he was now, he wanted to cry himself. He gave a discreet cough.

"Sara, perhaps your mother has need of the old healer?"

Sara looked up, realizing that she had forgotten the Tribune's existence. She knew he was probably right.

"Father," she pleaded. "What is wrong with Mother?"

Jubal looked past her to Abigail. "She has been that way since the day the two of you were taken away." He glared at Antonius. "She has lost all will to live."

Antonius swallowed hard, turning away. "Sara, go for the healer."

"He has already been here," Jubal told him. "There is nothing he can do."

Antonius jerked his head up. Where had he heard those words before? Is that what all physicians said?

Sara went to her mother, sitting beside her on the mat. "Let me talk to her. Alone, please."

Antonius nodded, but Jubal seemed disinclined to leave. Antonius motioned outside. "I need to speak to you," he told Jubal.

After they left, Sara took her mother's hand in her own. She started humming softly the song her mother used to sing to her when she was a child and afraid.

"Mother," she urged softly. Abigail opened her eyes again and smiled.

"Am I dreaming, Sara?"

"No, Mother. I have come home."

Abigail's face wrinkled into confusion. "I don't understand."

"The Tribune brought me home to see you. He has been very kind to me."

Sara went on to tell her mother about Diana and life at the villa. "So you see, Mother," she concluded, "God must want me there for a purpose. I haven't been harmed in any way. In fact, I have been treated as though I were a friend instead of a slave."

Abigail smiled. "I need to ask the Lord's forgiveness. I didn't trust Him to take care of you." She lifted a hand to stroke Sara's cheek. "If He has a purpose for you, then He must also have one for your brother."

"Yes, Mother," Sara choked. "And for you and Father as well."

When Jubal and Antonius came back, Antonius looked from Sara to her mother. "She is resting better now," she told both of them.

Antonius nodded. "Your father needs to speak to you. I will wait outside." He paused. "Better yet, I will allow you time with your family and I will come back for you later." He clicked his heels together, bowed, and left.

By the time Antonius had returned, Sara had managed to get her mother to eat some food. After all they had to say to each other, Sara knew that her parents would be okay now. Whatever Antonius had said to her father had brought the color back to his face and the pride back to his eyes. Sara had prayed with her mother and could tell it had brought her peace. Still, Sara was reluctant to leave them.

Sara was surprised when Antonius told her parents, "Sara may come and see you at least once a week."

Her mother had smiled then. It was the hardest thing Sara had ever had to do to walk away from her family just then, but she knew Antonius would never leave her behind. Because of Diana.

Antonius helped her into the chariot and took up the reins. Before he could snap the whip, Sara laid her hand over his. He looked at her questioningly.

"Tribune, I would like to see Ahaz before we leave."

"The healer?" he questioned.

Sara nodded her head. Antonius hesitated, but decided that

she must want to consult him because of her mother. He owed her that much.

"Show me the way."

Sara led him down the street and out past the village. They hadn't gone far when Sara motioned for him to stop. Antonius looked at the mud hut with distaste.

"Here?"

Sara nodded and started to get down from the chariot.

"I will go with you," he told her.

"No!"

Antonius pulled back in surprise, sudden suspicion bringing a frown to his face.

"Ahaz will not talk to me if you are there," she told him placatingly. She waited for his permission, looking everywhere but at him.

"Go, then," he snapped. "But be quick."

When Sara returned, she was clutching a bag in her hand. Antonius helped her into the chariot.

"What is that?" he wanted to know.

"Some things Ahaz gave me." Antonius stared at the bag doubtfully, so Sara placed the bag out of sight. "Ahaz has always shared with the people of my village the things that he grows. Herbs, spices, various plants."

"For medicines?"

"Sometimes," Sara replied. "Bacchus told me that he likes to experiment with various spices and herbs, so I thought I would bring him some."

Antonius grunted an answer, taking the reins in his hands and deftly applying the whip. They were silent on the return trip, each thinking their own thoughts.

Gallus took the reins from Antonius, who turned to help Sara alight from the chariot.

"Go and see how Diana is. I will be along in a minute."

Sara found Diana in much better spirits, though her face

was extremely pale.

"Oh Sara! I'm so glad you're home. Where's Antonius?"

"He said he would be here shortly," Sara told her.

"Please, Sara," Diana begged weakly. "Could you massage my scalp like you do? I have a fearful headache. If it wasn't so early, I'd take my sleeping draught now."

Sara frowned, but went to Diana and released the ivory bone pins from her elaborate hairdo. Slowly Sara began to massage her scalp, humming a tune as she did so. Sara could feel the tension begin to drain out of Diana. She was unaware of Antonius watching from the doorway.

"Oh, that feels good," Diana sighed. "You have magic hands."

Sara laughed. "I don't know about that, but my father used to enjoy me doing this for him."

"How was your family?" Diana wanted to know.

Sara sobered. "My mother was ill. My father. . .he seemed all right when we left."

Antonius entered the room and came to stand close beside Sara. She felt suddenly clumsy, though Diana didn't notice any difference.

Decimus knocked on the door. "My lady, the physician is here."

Sara felt Diana stiffen beneath her fingers. "You don't need to see him, if you don't want to," she told Diana.

"Of course she does," Antonius intervened. "If you can't be sensible, leave the room."

"Tribune. . ."

"I said, leave," he commanded, taking her by the arm and forcibly removing her from the room.

Sara paced up and down the balcony until the physician left. Going swiftly into the room, she found Diana much as she had previously. Sara's lips tightened when she saw the bandage where the physician had bled her again. Diana's eyes were glassy.

"Sara," she whispered. "I think I want to sleep now."

"Yes, Diana," she answered softly, her eyes filling with sympathy. "I will get things ready."

After Diana was asleep, Sara hurried to the vegetable garden behind the house where she knew she wouldn't be interrupted. Throwing herself to her knees, she began to pray fervently. She felt a measure of peace when she finished, her eyes swimming with tears as she lifted them to the dusky sky.

When Diana was asleep, Sara was free to do as she chose. Tonight, however, something told her to stay close to Diana, so she busied herself picking up in Diana's room. When she finished, she pulled a chair close to the bed, leaving one lamp lit so that she could see if Diana needed her.

How long Sara had been sitting there she didn't know, but darkness had veiled the night with its cloak. Crickets began to chirp in the peristyle below, their familiar cadences seeping in through the open door. The night was warm and very little air came into the room. Diana became restless, moving her head from side to side. She started to moan softly, becoming even more agitated. Sara got up and leaned over her, putting a hand to her cheek. Diana's skin was extremely hot.

Sara went out to the balcony and called Decimus. He must have been close by because he was by her side almost instantly.

"What is it, Sara?"

"Diana has a fever," she told him and noticed that worry lines creased his brow. "I need some cool water."

"I'll get it right away."

Sara hurried back to Diana. She felt her forehead and became instantly worried herself. Her fever was climbing.

Decimus entered the room with a bowl of water and brought it to Sara. "How is she?"

"Not good. Her fever is getting worse and so is her restlessness. If she gets worse, she may harm herself flailing about like she is."

Decimus left the room and came back quickly, carrying a soft drape of material. He found Sara trying to hold Diana down. Taking the material, he wrapped Diana in its folds tightly, which only caused her to become more agitated.

"Antonius! Antonius!" she rasped.

"What should we do, Decimus?"

Decimus stood worrying his bottom lip with his teeth. "I think I had better go for the master. He left word with Abijah where he would be in case anything happened." His voice lowered. "I have never seen her this bad before."

Sara hesitated. She couldn't handle Diana alone, she hadn't the strength. In her delirium Diana possessed surprising strength herself. "I think we should send Abijah. I need you to help me with Diana."

"Abijah is not here right now. He went to his brother's house, but he told me where to find the Tribune."

"I will go then," Sara told him, but Decimus was already shaking his head. Diana fought the covers, managing to get her legs free and kicking out angrily. It took all Decimus had to wrap her snugly again. He looked at Sara worriedly.

"Perhaps you are right, but if you go out at night alone, the master will have my hide."

"What choice do we have?" she remonstrated with him. "I don't have time to argue with you. Tell me where to find the Tribune."

Sara found herself hurrying through the dark streets of Ephesus, praying wildly as she flew along. Her prayers were answered because she reached the house she was looking for unmolested. She only had time to take in the fact that this villa was almost as large as Antonius'. Pushing through the gates, she climbed her way to the door, pounding furiously upon its solid wooden surface. She waited breathlessly until she heard a sound from the other side.

The door opened slightly and light spilled out into the darkened courtyard. A servant peered out, trying to focus on Sara's darkened figure. His eyes squinted slightly, his face drawing into a frown when he realized the woman before him must be a servant.

"What do you want?" he growled, inching the door closed to a mere crack.

Sara released a breath, wringing her hands in the folds of her tunic. "Is Antonius Severus here?"

Recognition flashed momentarily in the servant's eyes, but he made no answer. His mistress had made it quite plain that nothing was to interfere with her party, especially not where Antonius Severus was concerned.

"Please," Sara begged. "I have to see him. His sister is very ill."

The servant opened the door wider, torn by his desire to please his mistress and the sure knowledge that Antonius would have him flayed if he ever found out that he had refused to bring him knowledge of his sister. As he stood hesitating, a figure approached from the street, stopping when he recognized Sara.

"Sara? What are you doing here?"

Sara turned to him with relief. "Tribune Flavius, I must speak with Antonius. He left word with Abijah that he would be here."

Flavius was instantly alert, his eyes searching her face. "Is it Diana?"

"She's very ill. Her fever is making her delirious and she continually calls for Antonius."

Face pale, Flavius turned to the servant. "What are you waiting for?" he snapped. "Get Antonius!"

"Yes, my lord."

Flavius waited with Sara, watching the man's back disappear into the anteroom where Helena held her parties.

"How bad is she?" he asked quietly, and Sara could hear the desolation in his voice. He must love Diana very much. She wondered if Diana knew.

Antonius appeared, quickly covering the distance to where they stood. A beautiful redhead followed in his wake, clutching his arm when he would have left.

"Antonius! Where are you going?" she demanded petulantly.

"I'm sorry, Helena. I must go to my sister."

"For the love of Poseidon, why must you always attend your sister? What good will it do? She's going to die anyway."

Sara was shocked at such coldness, especially coming from one with such flawless beauty. She saw Antonius' eyes darken with his anger. He shook her hand off as though she were some vile thing. Sara could see that Tribune Flavius was just as outraged, his fists curling at his sides. Antonius would have left without a word, except that Helena tried once more.

"I'm sorry, Antonius," she told him in her most seductive voice. "I didn't mean it. It's just that I have missed you so much." She stroked her hands up his arms and curled them around his neck. Antonius remained still, his arms hanging at his sides.

Helena's full red lips curled into a pout. "Oh, Antonius. You have become such a bore lately."

Reaching up, Antonius removed her hands from his body, and gave her a slight shove. "In that case, Helena, I will not bother you with my presence ever again."

Antonius took Sara by the arm and pulled her down the steps. Sara could hear Flavius turn to follow them. He looked over his shoulder and gave Helena one final parting shot.

"The same goes for me, Helena."

When they reached the street, they could hear Helena's angry voice.

"You'll be back, Antonius."

Antonius and Flavius exchanged glances. Flavius shrugged his shoulders, a grin splitting his features. "I feel like a fly that has just had a narrow escape from a spider."

Antonius nodded his head in agreement, but his attention had already turned towards Sara.

"What's happened?"

Taking a breath, Sara explained Diana's condition. Antonius listened in silence, his face becoming a grave mask. "Flavius, will you go for the physician? Tell him it's urgent."

Flavius saluted once, then disappeared in the opposite direction, his figure quickly swallowed up by the darkness. Sara was panting trying to keep up with Antonius, but she said nothing. She was just as anxious as Antonius to reach the villa.

Antonius went quickly to Diana's room and found Decimus kneeling beside the bed.

"Decimus?"

The boy jumped quickly to his feet. "My lord," he sighed with relief. "She is still burning with fever. I have bathed her face constantly, and that seems to soothe her some, but she continually calls for you. I have never seen her this bad before."

Antonius sat down on the bed, pulling the wrap from Diana's body. Taking her firmly into his arms, he held her tightly and began to talk to her soothingly. Slowly she started to relax until her head rested against his shoulder, her eyes closed.

Decimus moved by Sara to fetch more water. She laid a hand on his arm.

"Decimus? You were praying?" she asked him in a soft whisper.

He looked at her in surprise. "Yes, my lady."

"May I ask in whose name you were offering for Diana's life?"

Decimus pressed his lips together, straightening his shoulders. "I asked in Jesus' name," he answered her just as quietly.

Sara smiled at him then, her eyes locking with his. "His will be done," she agreed. They stared at each other several seconds, probing each other with their eyes, realizing that they had a common bond.

At a sound below, they turned to see Flavius ascending the stairs rapidly, the physician following in his steps. Sara felt her heart sink at the sight of the rotund man. She disliked him intensely, realizing that some of her dislike stemmed from her own prejudice. He was nothing like Ahaz. Ahaz cared for the people he ministered to. This man did little and charged exorbitant prices.

The physician pushed past Sara and Decimus, going to stand beside Antonius. He pulled back Diana's eyelids and let them drop back into place. He was silent a long time. Finally he spoke.

"She's too far gone," he told Antonius. "There's only one thing left for me to do."

seven

The silence in the room was almost oppressive as each person tried to take in what the physician was trying to say. Sara's eyes widened in alarm. She didn't trust this physician.

"What can you do?" Antonius asked him quietly, his eyes never leaving Diana's prostrate form. He cuddled her gently, burying his face in her golden hair.

"I can make a mixture of hemlock and allow her to die quietly and peacefully." There was a total lack of emotion in the physician's voice.

"No!" Four voices rose in unison, making the one word thunder through the room. The physician jumped in surprise.

"She would feel no pain," he told them placatingly. "She is so far gone now that she probably doesn't even know what's going on around her."

"My lord," Decimus begged. "You cannot allow this!"

Sara's eyes burned with her anger, but she said nothing, allowing Antonius time to think. Surely he would not consider such a suggestion.

Flavius stepped closer to Antonius, reaching out a hand to Diana and running his fingers through her hair. His eyes roved her face, but he addressed himself to Antonius. "Think carefully, my friend. Life is too precious to be taken lightly."

If anyone knew that, it was Antonius. Even though he was a trained soldier, he still had a hard time taking a life.

"I know what you are saying, but I have to think of Diana."

"Tribune," Sara interrupted. "Surely there is another way."

Antonius stared at her in anger. "What would you suggest? Praying to that caring God of yours?"

72

The physician started to unpack his bag. "There is one more thing I might try," he told Antonius. Antonius' eyes filled with hope. "I can try to bleed her heavier. If I remove enough fluid, then perhaps her humors will come into alignment."

Antonius laid Diana back against the bed. He stared at her a long time before he finally stood and began pacing back and forth. He knew little about medicine and what he had seen so far had not impressed him. But either way, Diana was going to die. Pain like he hadn't experienced since his parents' death many years ago clutched at his heart. He had been the sole caretaker for Diana since she was twelve years old. Had it only been five years since his parents' death? It seemed so much longer. He felt much older than his thirty years.

Sara placed an urgent hand against his forearm. "Please, Tribune. Don't let them bleed her anymore."

"You have a better suggestion?" he snapped, jerking his arm from her.

She answered him quietly but firmly. "Our Scriptures teach that life is in the blood. As a soldier, surely you know that to be true."

Antonius hesitated. What she said made sense. When a soldier was weak, you tried to stop his bleeding, not inflict more. Still, Xanthus was one of the finest physicians in Rome.

"My lord, I must protest." Xanthus threw Sara a murderous glance. "I am trying to keep her alive. What does a plebeian know of medicine?"

Forgetting her position, Sara whirled towards him, her eyes shooting brown sparks. "You are killing her! You with your rich foods and bloodletting. You care not for Diana. You care only for your fat purse!"

"Sara!" Antonius' eyes told her more than words that she had gone too far. Concluding that punishment was inevitable, she decided she had nothing to lose.

"Please, Antonius," she begged. "Let me care for her."

Antonius was as much surprised by Sara's use of his name as the fact that she disobeyed his order for silence. Xanthus drew himself up angrily, spearing Sara with a daggered glance.

"You? What do you know about medicine?" he asked her scathingly.

"He has said she will die anyway," Sara gritted. "What is there to lose?"

"I'll tell you what there is to lose," Xanthus argued. "The difference between dying with dignity and dying without pain."

"Enough!" Antonius thundered, and Sara knew better than to disobey. She must let him decide for himself. His strong will and arrogant pride would never allow him to submit to a woman if he felt backed into a corner.

"Take Decimus and go to the garden," he told her quietly.

Her eyes pleaded with him, but he turned away. Sara would have liked to slap the smirk from the physician's face. Dropping her head, she quietly left the room, Decimus close on her heels.

"Flavius, take the physician to the bibliotheca and show him some of my manuscripts. I'll be along shortly."

"Of course. This way."

Xanthus would have argued, but the strange glitter in Tribune Flavius' eyes kept him silent. He could feel the rage emanating from the young soldier.

When Antonius was alone with Diana he sat down beside her on the bed. She was so still. So pale. She looked as though a breath of wind would blow her away. He frowned. She hadn't seemed so just this morning. She had seemed lively, anticipating a visit from Flavius. Could Sara be right? He remembered how quickly Sara's wound had healed. Was that why she had stopped to see the old healer today? Could she have been seeking his advice?

One thing was for certain. Xanthus had no love for Diana and Sara did.

❧

When Sara left Diana's room, her eyes were filled with tears. Decimus came up behind her and laid a hand on her shoulder.

"He will not do it."

Sara wished she could feel as certain. "How can you be so sure?"

"I know him. He's not capable of such a thing."

Sara sighed, lifting her eyes to the stars. "Decimus, Satan has many ways of making something evil seem right."

"Then let us pray together that our Lord Jesus will not allow Satan to so deceive Tribune Antonius," he answered confidently.

For several moments, all was quiet in the garden except for the soft petitioning voices of both Sara and Decimus. As always when Sara took her troubles to the Lord, she felt a sense of peace envelop her. When they had finished praying, Decimus led Sara to the seat near the fountain. He sat down next to her, folding his hands between his legs. His head drooped and he stared somberly at the ground.

"You love Diana, don't you?" Sara asked him softly.

He nodded his head. "But not in the way you think. When I was brought to Ephesus as a captive seven years ago, I was only ten years old. The master's parents were alive then." He paused, picking a dried flower petal from the ground and twirling it through his fingers. "My lady was also ten at the time. Her father had come to the market to purchase a slave. He wanted someone strong. A man. My lady noticed me among the others and felt sorry for me. She pleaded with her father to choose me." Here he stopped, a grin spreading across his face at the memory. "Her father could refuse her nothing. She was the light of his life. So. . .here I am."

Sara smiled. She could imagine Diana being imperative and spoiled even at that age. "You became friends?"

Decimus nodded again. "She was the sister I left behind," he told her quietly.

All was peaceful and quiet in the garden save for the rushing water of the fountain. Sara looked up at Diana's door. It was hard to imagine that only a few feet away, a battle was going on for the soul of a young girl. Sara began to pray harder.

When Antonius entered the library he found Xanthus warily watching Flavius, who was twisting his dagger in his hands. Antonius hid a grin. Flavius was making his feelings all too apparent.

"Flavius, will you bring Sara to me? And you may as well bring Decimus too."

Flavius sheathed his dagger with an extra loud snap and left the room. Before long he returned, Sara and Decimus close behind. They searched Antonius' face for some clue to his decision, but found none.

"Xanthus," Antonius began. "I respect your profession and have been pleased with your services," he lied, "but I have decided to allow my sister to die on her own." He swallowed hard.

Sara went limp with relief. *Thank you, Lord*!

The physician nodded his head in understanding. Not many people would choose such a hard way, but some simply could not let go. This he understood and he found no offense.

"If you need me further, Tribune, you have only to call."

"Thank you." Antonius raised an eyebrow at Decimus, who interpreted his look correctly. "Will you see that Xanthus receives his payment?"

"Yes, my Lord."

When they left the room, Antonius turned to Sara. "If there's anything you can do, do it. But I want you to understand that if she dies painfully I will hold you personally responsible."

"I understand. May I have total responsibility for Diana? Her diet, everything?"

Antonius sighed, pushing his hands through his hair. He looked at Flavius, who looked just as intently back at him. He nodded his head. As Sara was about to leave the room, Antonius took her by the arm. Although he held her lightly, his hand felt like a shackle of steel, his eyes menacing in their severity. "Remember what I said. I don't want her to suffer."

"I love her, too," she reminded him quietly and he loosened his hold. Nodding her head at Flavius, she left the room.

≈

Sara made a mixture from the herbs Ahaz had given her and added it to a bowl of water. After mixing it together, she then tried to spoon some into Diana's mouth. Little by little, the brew went down her throat. Taking a cloth, she dipped it into the cool water Decimus had brought for her and placed it on Diana's forehead. She then settled herself in a chair beside the bed, prepared for a long night's vigil.

Periodically throughout the night, Diana would become restless and start to moan, rolling her head back and forth. Sara would then give her more of the herb mixture and replace the compress with a cool one. Then Diana would settle down again for several hours.

The sun was beginning to send its first fingers of light into the semi-dark room when Sara's head started to nod. Diana hadn't awakened in hours. Head dropping to her chest, Sara jerked awake. Blinking sleepy eyes, she got up and went to Diana, laying a hand against her cheek. Her breathing was deep and regular, and Sara could tell the fever had broken and the worst was over.

She opened the drapes wide to let in the morning light, knowing that it wouldn't bother Diana. Her sleep was too sound. The herbs Ahaz had given her had helped to alleviate the fever, but she wouldn't mention them to Antonius. She sensed that he would not approve.

Antonius had left word that he would sleep in the room next to Diana's and that he should be called if there was any change. Sara went to the door and found Decimus asleep on the balcony in front of the threshold. She smiled softly. Let the boy sleep. She would go to Antonius herself.

Stepping over the sleeping lad, Sara stepped carefully and quietly to the next door. She tapped lightly, but got no response. Opening the door slowly, she found Antonius asleep still sitting up on the couch, his head drooped to one side and his dark hair spilling across his forehead. He looked so childishly innocent that Sara felt her heart melt at the sight of him. Crossing the room, she lightly touched his shoulder.

In one quick movement, she found herself pinned beneath him on the couch, his eyes glittering strangely down into hers. Her eyes opened wide in fear, her heart pounding loudly in her chest.

"Tribune!" she squealed in fright. "It's Sara!"

For a moment his eyes remained unfocused, then slowly he relaxed. He shook his head slightly to clear it, releasing her wrist from his crushing grip.

"Sara?" He looked down into her face, one part of his mind registering the fear he saw there. "Sara." His voice softened and he lifted a hand to stroke down her cheek. Her wide eyes stared back at him, and Antonius felt himself move as if in a dream. He lowered his head, bringing his lips softly down on hers.

The moment his lips touched hers, Sara felt her mind begin

to spin. Without realizing it, she returned his kiss, her lips telling him of her innocence. Antonius knew he should have pulled back, but a strange fire was beginning to warm his blood. He pressed closer, his lips becoming more demanding.

Warning bells went off in Sara's mind. She tried to push Antonius away, but his strength was too much for her. She tried to turn her head away, but found herself unable to move. Using the only weapon available to her, she began to fervently pray.

"My lord?" Decimus' voice from the doorway brought Antonius back from the yawning precipice he had so nearly tumbled into. He pulled back quickly, running a hand through his hair in agitation.

"Sara!" Antonius was at a loss for words. He leaned back, and Sara hastily climbed from the couch. She would have just as hastily exited the room, but Antonius stopped her.

"Wait!" Sara froze with her back still to him. "What is it, Decimus?" he wanted to know.

Decimus glanced from one to the other, casting his eyes to the floor. "I was looking for Sara," he answered quietly. "I couldn't find her in my lady's room and wanted to find out how my lady was doing."

Both men fixed their attention on Sara. "The fever has broken and she is sleeping quietly. That is what I came to tell you, Tribune." Sara's eyes were also cast downward, but flew up at Decimus' whoop of joy. She had to smile when she saw the joy that radiated from his face.

"I will go and bring you something to eat," he told her happily, skipping across the balcony.

Sara would have followed, but again Antonius stopped her. "I would have a word with you." She heard him move behind her and felt herself tense. Antonius saw her body stiffen and clenched his jaw in frustration.

"Sara." He laid a hand on her shoulder and felt her jump

slightly. Gritting his teeth, he dropped his hand. "I'm sorry about what happened just now. I didn't know what I was doing. I would never hurt you. Surely you know that."

She didn't answer him for a moment and when she did, it was to change the subject. "Diana is much better this morning. Her fever is gone and she was sleeping peacefully when I left."

"I heard you tell Decimus."

"Is there anything else, Tribune?"

Antonius sighed, turning away. "Not for the moment. I will be along to see Diana as soon as I have visited the baths and cleaned up some."

"Yes, Tribune."

For the rest of the day Sara attended to Diana. Her lack of sleep was beginning to tell on her and she started to droop wearily. Decimus found her patting water onto her face to keep awake and convinced her to lay down on the other sleeping couch to rest. At first she protested, but when Decimus told her he would stay in the room also, she relented. Within moments she was asleep.

Although Diana awakened periodically, she was awake for only minutes at a time. Sara knew that what her body needed the most was time to recuperate from all the bloodletting, so she didn't worry too much about Diana's diet. She did, however, send word to Bacchus to prepare some broth for Diana's nourishment. Decimus returned with a tray holding a bowl of broth and resting in a small urn was a blue hyacinth. Sara laughed aloud.

"What is so funny?" Decimus was clearly puzzled.

"Bacchus is letting me know that he approves of Diana's diet," Sara told him.

Decimus raised an eyebrow, clearly unconvinced. "I hope this works."

Sara took his face between her hands and smiled into his

eyes. "What I want from you, my brother, is your faithful prayers."

He grinned back at her. "I have never stopped."

Releasing him, she stepped back. "Someday, Decimus, I would like to learn how you came to know the Lord."

"And I you."

They smiled at each other before parting company and although Decimus stayed close by, Sara had no need of him again that day.

The next three days followed a pattern. Diana would awaken periodically and Sara would give her some broth, bathe her, brush her hair and let her go back to sleep. Antonius would come in the evening to check up on her, and Sara's heart never failed to miss a beat whenever he entered the room.

He would sit and hold Diana's hand, even when she was asleep, and talk to her about many things. Sometimes he would bring some of his Greek manuscripts and read her poetry. Sara would sit enthralled, though she didn't think anything could compare with the psalms of David.

Color was beginning to come back to Diana's cheeks and Sara attributed that to Bacchus' cooking. He truly did know how to feed an invalid.

Five days after Diana's collapse, she opened her eyes and they regarded Sara clearly for the first time.

"What time is it?" she asked, trying to lift herself up on the bed pillows.

Sara hurried to her side. "You must stay put. You have been very ill."

"Have I? Where's Antonius?"

"I'm not sure, but he's here in the villa somewhere. Do you want me to send for him?"

Diana lay back down. "Not right now. For some reason I'm famished."

Sara smiled with pleasure. "That is wonderful news. What would you like to eat?"

"I'm so hungry I could eat Orion," she joked.

Sara's trill of laughter reached Antonius, who was coming up the steps. He hurried the rest of the way, entering Diana's room and almost knocking Sara over. He grabbed her arms to keep her from falling, clenching his teeth when she jerked away.

"Tribune," she told him in a breathless voice, "Diana is much better this morning."

"So I can see." He smiled widely at Diana, going over and sitting on the couch beside her. She was almost emaciated, bones protruding from her shoulders. "We have Sara to thank for your life," he told her.

Diana looked from one to the other. "Someone will have to tell me what has happened. I seem to be missing something."

For the rest of the day, Diana spent her time between eating and periods of sleep. She was better than Antonius had seen her in a long while, and he thrilled at her increasing intervals of wakefulness.

Whenever he tried to express his appreciation to Sara, she would mumble something about her God and flee. With rising irritation, Antonius realized that if he wanted to have a conversation with Sara, he was going to have to demand her presence in some way. A stubborn light came into his eyes, and his shoulders straightened with assumed arrogance. So be it.

eight

"Antonius?"

"Hmm?" Antonius raised his eyes reluctantly from the scroll he was perusing. He glanced at his sister, noting with pleasure that she had lost much of her skeletal appearance and was beginning to fill out healthily. *Sara's doing, no doubt.* Since she had taken over Diana's care, Sara had been as bristly as a bear.

He remembered bringing Diana a special delicacy of hummingbird tongues only to be faced by a wrathful Sara reminding him of his promise to allow her complete control of Diana's care, including her diet. At first he had been angry, then amused. He certainly couldn't fault the results.

His sister's bright blue eyes stared out at him from a beautiful face framed by the gold of her now full and shiny hair. She worried her bottom lip with perfect white teeth.

"What do you think of Sara and Decimus' God? Do you think it's possible there could really be only one God and that He really cares about His people?"

Antonius frowned. "Now what's going on inside that pretty little head of yours? What brought this on?"

She wrinkled her nose, turning her attention out the window. The day was beautiful, and the cobalt blue of the sky was an almost exact duplicate of the eyes studying it. Diana regarded the vivid colors of the warm morning solemnly.

"I almost died, Antonius," she told him softly.

He felt fear clutch his heart as he remembered that night. Diana was the one person he loved most in all the world, and he had almost lost her. So many happy memories linked them inextricably together.

"I would have thought that would make you all the more grateful to be alive. Ready to live your life to the fullest."

Diana turned her gaze back to him and regarded him solemnly. "If I had died, Antonius, where would I be now?"

Antonius got impatiently to his feet, brushing a hand haphazardly through his hair. He began to pace to and fro.

"What do you want me to say?"

Diana sighed gently. "You have so much knowledge at your fingertips, and yet you can't answer such a simple question."

"Simple!" He blew out his breath in frustration. "Man has studied that question since the beginning of time."

"And?"

"Diana!" He paused, struggling for an answer. His mind seemed to go blank. "What do you think?"

"I think you're trying to throw this back on me," she grinned. "I'm not the one who spends hours poring over dusty old manuscripts." Diana watched through prideful eyes of love how Antonius was struggling to give her a satisfactory answer. He had always been her mentor. So calm and sure in a crisis, yet here he was floundering over a theological issue.

"Sara and Decimus have both told me of their belief in a place called Heaven for the saved, and hell for the unsaved."

Antonius glared at her in aggravation. "Well, I wouldn't put too much faith in their religion. Their leader was a carpenter who was nailed to a cross."

"They told me this also," she answered softly.

"If He were a god, how could this happen?" he remonstrated logically.

"They say He allowed Himself to die for our sins, so that

we could live forever with God."

"What utter nonsense!" Antonius would have a word with Sara and Decimus when they returned from visiting Sara's parents. "Listen to me, love," Antonius' voice was soft with reassurance. "What grievous sins could you have committed to warrant eternal punishment? You've always been kind and loving."

"But it's more than that," she told him, and he rolled his eyes heavenward.

"For the love of Poseidon! Can we change the subject?" he begged.

Diana watched her brother, her lips twitching with amusement. He looked like a caged lion, and just about as approachable.

"I'm hungry," she acquiesced, and grinned openly when he sighed with relief.

"I'll tell Beatrice to bring us a tray," he told her, hurrying through the door.

When Beatrice returned with the tray, Antonius glanced over it skeptically. How could Diana be gaining weight and health from such a selection of food? He set the tray down on the marble table next to Diana's couch, raising an inquiring brow.

"There doesn't seem to be much of sustenance," he grumbled.

Diana laughed joyously. "Oh, Antonius, if you could only see your face. Sit down and let's eat. I'm starved!"

Shaking his head, Antonius sat down across from her. He bit into the delicately seasoned fish, chewing slowly. His eyebrows winged upwards.

"This is really good!" he said in surprise.

Diana said nothing, merely handing him portions of the fruit mixture and nuts. Her eyes danced merrily as she watched her brother consume his food with obvious enjoyment.

"Here, try these. They're my favorite." She handed him a small cake and watched his eyes widen in surprise when he bit into it.

"What's in this thing? It's delicious."

Diana sucked the honey from her own fingers before answering. "Chopped dates, almonds, honey, things like that."

She reached across, dabbing at the honey dripping down his chin. This was almost like the time they were children and she and Antonius had gone on a picnic.

"So my brother, what are you studying today?" She indicated the scrolls he had been studying earlier. Diana wondered at the sudden color that rushed to his face. Antonius turned his eyes away before answering, thereby missing the grin his sister threw his way.

"Actually, I've been reading some of the writings of Josephus."

"And who is Josephus?"

"Josephus is a Jewish historian and statesman."

"Ah."

Antonius noticed the grin and frowned. "Don't look at me like that."

"Like what?" Diana asked innocently.

"Oh, never mind," he answered in exasperation, wiping his hands on the wet towel provided, and rising to his feet.

"Where are you going?"

"I have work to do," he told her gruffly.

Diana's eyes darkened and the smile left her face. "You said you would keep me company until Sara returned," she pouted.

"Diana," he answered her softly. "You don't need me to stay with you. You are well now, both physically and mentally."

"But I get so bored," she complained. "Sitting here day in and day out. I still can't walk!"

Brushing a hand through her hair, he tugged gently,

forcing her to look at his face. "That will come with time."

"But I'll go crazy here alone. I have nothing to do."

Antonius thought for a minute. "How about if I carry you out to the peristyle? You could sit in the shade by the fountain. Would you like that?"

"Oh yes!"

Antonius had to smile at her childlike enthusiasm. Reaching down, he lifted her effortlessly into his strong arms and carried her down the steps to the garden. Settling her comfortably on the bench, he called for Beatrice.

Beatrice came quickly at his call, lifting her eyes demurely to his. What he read in her eyes was anything but demure. Frowning, he brusquely instructed her to see to Diana's needs, then quickly turned on his heel and left. The purple trim from his short tunic gave color to the otherwise white robe. His skin was burnished by the sun, as was most of the Roman legion, and his build was that of an athlete. Many a heart had been lost at the altar of this young Roman. Two pair of female eyes watched him stride away; one brown pair with regret, the other pair with amusement.

"I'll call you if I need you, Beatrice," Diana told the girl.

"Yes, my lady."

Diana leaned her head back, basking in the warmth of the sun shining down through the peristyle roof. Eyes closed, she smiled at the feeling of euphoria that enveloped her. Why had she not thought to come here before? For a long while she sat thus, enjoying the freedom from the monotony of her room. She had missed so much the last several months holing herself up in her room. Refusing to live because Ledo had died. Strange, she could barely remember his face. How could this be if she was so much in love?

"Surely the goddess Aphrodite has chosen to descend from Mount Olympus and grace the earth with her beauty. My eyes are blinded by such a radiant vision."

Diana had jumped at the first word, her heart thumping with fright. She turned now to greet her visitor, a smile blazoned across her face.

"Flavius! You flatterer. You scared me half to death."

"That wasn't my intention," he assured her. "But seeing you sitting here. So lovely, so. . .alive."

Diana laughed. "Oh, Flavius! It does feel good to be among the living again!" She cocked her head to one side. "But if you are looking for Antonius, he has gone to his office."

Flavius' voice came back soft and low. "No, I didn't come to see Antonius. I heard you were almost well again and I had to come see for myself." His voice became husky. "You are more beautiful than ever."

Color flooded Diana's cheeks and she turned her head away. "So what is happening in the legion? Are you still to remain in Ephesus, or will they be sending you elsewhere?"

Flavius sat down beside her, staring at the water tumbling in the fountain. "I have decided to resign my commission," he told her, and her eyes widened in surprise.

"Why?"

He glanced sideways at her, his eyes dark and unfathomable. "A legionary cannot marry, and I have a desire to do so."

Diana felt the color drain from her face. Turning away from him, she clutched the front of her palla, closing her eyes against the pain.

"How nice," she told him, and was surprised that her voice sounded so normal. "As for me, I plan never to marry," she told him airily, and missed the hurt that flashed through his eyes. "I could never leave Antonius."

"But. . .surely someday Antonius will want to marry?"

"Who will want to marry?" Antonius asked as he walked into the garden, catching the last of the conversation. "What am I missing here?"

Flavius rose to his feet. "Nothing," he answered quietly. "We were just discussing marriage."

"Whose? "Antonius wanted to know.

"Never mind," Diana told him quickly, and Antonius' eyes narrowed when he noticed her pale face. "I'm tired, Antonius. Could you carry me back up to my room?"

"Allow me." Flavius reached down and lifted her into his arms. Biting her lip, Diana turned her face away from Flavius. She could feel the pounding of his heart and realized that, in a way, she affected him as he did her. But now he was to marry. He had said nothing to her. Perhaps he had confided in Antonius. For years now she had considered Flavius a special friend, but it hadn't occurred to her until now just how much she had grown to love him. He had always treated her with gentle respect, much like Antonius treated her. Tears shimmered in her eyes. Suddenly, she no longer wished to be treated like a sister, but she couldn't tell Flavius that. He would feel awkward to know that she had fallen in love with him.

Setting her down on the couch, Flavius leaned towards Diana, his eyes searching hers. Diana sighed in relief when Antonius walked in the door.

"Is there anything you want me to do for you, Diana?" Antonius asked.

"If you would close the drapes for me, I think I would like to take a nap."

Doing as she asked, Antonius then walked to the door, motioning for Flavius to follow. Reluctantly, Flavius backed towards the door, his eyes never leaving Diana's face. Pivoting abruptly, he left, and Diana could hear his sandals clicking against the concrete. Burying her face in her pillow, she wept bitterly.

❧

Sara reached up her hand and gently touched the mezuzah on

the doorpost before entering her parents' house. She walked across the dirt floor to the three sitting on mats at the low table.

"You found Ahaz well?" Abigail asked her.

Sara grinned. "Have you ever known him to be otherwise? He gave me more herbs and spices." She held up the bag for their inspection.

Decimus turned to Jubal. "If not for Sara, Diana would have died. God worked a miracle through her."

Jubal nodded his grizzled head. "Some good has come from this situation."

Sarah smiled at him and looked at her mother. "I wish you could meet Diana. She really is a wonderful person. And so beautiful."

"King Saul was a handsome man, and look what happened to him. Beauty of the heart is what matters," Abigail answered.

Decimus was staring hard at Sara before he turned to her mother. "I must agree."

Sara smiled wryly at them. "I know what you are saying, but it would be nice to have beauty such as Diana."

"Pshaw," her father snorted. "What does a Roman who is willing to own slaves know of beauty?"

"Father," Sara argued. "It was forcefully brought to my attention that in times past when the Israelites were conquerors, they owned slaves also."

Her father glowered at her, but couldn't argue the point. Sara had been unable to either when Antonius first brought it to her attention. "To the victors go the spoils," he had told her.

Decimus broke into her musings. "We need to get back soon."

Sara nodded her head in agreement. Darkness would soon descend and it wouldn't be good to be caught on the roads after dark.

Decimus stood to his feet while Sara kissed her mother goodbye. Jubal and Abigail followed them out to the end of the road.

"I'm glad the Tribune kept his word," Jubal told Sara. "It's made all the difference in the world, being able to see for ourselves that you haven't suffered."

Sara's eyes filled with tears. "Keep praying for Diana."

"We will," Abigail answered for her husband. She hesitated a moment before laying a hand on the side of the cart. "Sara, if you could find out anything about Dathan. . ."

"I'll try, mother." Abigail stepped back from the cart, nodding her head. It was all Sara could do.

Decimus clicked to the horse and they were off, Sara watching until her parents were a mere speck in the distance. Decimus didn't miss the sheen in her soft brown eyes.

"I liked your parents."

Sara gave him a wobbly smile. "Yes, they are the best parents a girl could have."

A distant look came to Decimus' eyes as he stared off in the distance at the rising columns of Ephesus. "I wish I could remember more about my parents."

"Do you ever want to go back?"

"To Britannia?"

Sara nodded.

"I used to think about it a lot. Now. . .I don't know. It's been seven years since I've seen my parents and my home. I don't even know if they are still alive."

Sara felt sorry for him. At least she still had her parents, and with Antonius' kindness was able to visit them often. She thought she would have died if she had been in Decimus' place.

Thinking to lighten the mood, Sara smiled coyly at Decimus. "And is there another reason you are reluctant to leave? A girl perhaps?"

He glanced at her sharply before turning back to the road. Color mounted to his cheeks and Sara grinned.

"Aha! I thought so. Who is she?"

Decimus remained silent so Sara began to guess. "Bithnia? No? How about Beatrice?"

Decimus threw her a look of such scorn that Sara burst into laughter. The rest of the journey they teased each other back and forth, laughing gaily at one another's jokes. Decimus pulled the cart into the courtyard, laughingly lifting Sara out beside him.

Antonius saw them from the window of the bath room. He leaned against the sill, his eyes narrowed. Decimus still hadn't removed his hands from Sara's waist, and she was still laughing at something he had said. Antonius watched them broodingly, his thoughts far from pleasant.

Drying himself, he quickly put on a clean tunic, deciding to leave off the toga. He needed to talk to Sara about Diana. About this religious thing. When they entered the atrium, Antonius was waiting.

"I wish to speak with you, Sara."

Sara glanced at Decimus, who shrugged his shoulders, his eyes suddenly filled with worry. Sara followed Antonius through the atrium to the bibliotheca. This seemed to be his favorite room in the house, and Sara realized that it was probably due to his thirst for knowledge. He was forever studying the scrolls in the library and purchasing new ones to pore over in his leisure.

He stood still in the doorway, motioning for her to precede him. To do so would bring her in close proximity to his body. She stopped, unable to bring herself to move forward.

"Sara?"

Her eyes flew to his and she could see the amusement lurking there. The man knew the effect he had on her and was deliberately testing her will. Lifting her chin a notch,

Sara looked straight ahead and passed through the doorway, brushing against his chest as she did so. When her eyes went to his again, his were veiled, all traces of laughter gone.

Swallowing hard, Sara turned to address him. "Yes, Tribune?"

Antonius forgot what he had intended to say. Suddenly, the whole religion issue seemed so trivial. A look of irritation crossed his features.

"Why must you always call me Tribune?"

Sara looked at him in surprise. "But that's who you are."

"You called me Antonius once." His husky voice sent shivers up Sara's back even as hot color flooded her face.

"I didn't mean to. I. . .I forgot myself for a moment. It was not appropriate and I hope you will forgive me."

There was no denying the earnestness of the plea. Antonius nodded his head slightly in affirmation, his mind not completely on what she had just said. "Then why do you not call me master?" he demanded softly.

Sara dropped her eyes to the floor. "I have only one master."

She heard him move, but kept her eyes fixed on the blue inlaid design of the marble. Antonius reached out, placing a palm against her cheek, lifting her chin none too gently with his thumb. Sara quailed beneath his look. His eyes glittered dangerously, and Sara's heart started to pound in response, her eyes widening in alarm.

"Who, Sara, do you consider your master?" he asked in a softly ominous voice.

Sara had to swallow twice before she could answer. She realized how fiercely possessive Antonius could be about things he considered his. Take Orion for instance, or even Diana. But it had never occurred to her that he might become angry over a slave.

"My Lord, Jesus Christ, is the only man I will ever consider my master," she told him in a quavery voice.

She watched the dawning comprehension on his face and felt the tension leave his body. A slight smile quirked his lips to one side.

"Ah, I remember now. Your religion." His eyes roved her face before settling on her parted lips. Her chest rose and fell rapidly with a mixture of fear and her awareness of him as a man. "I have no problem with you worshipping your God in any way you choose. Just remember one thing. You belong to me." He punctuated each of the last four words by tapping her lips with his thumb.

Sara's lips thinned with anger. Jerking herself free, she stepped away from Antonius. She saw his face tighten with returning anger.

"Is that all you wished to talk to me about, Tribune?"

"No." He stared at her silently, his blue eyes smoldering in his anger. "What is going on between you and Decimus?"

Sara's head flew upwards and she gaped at him in complete shock. "Decimus?" She frowned, struggling to find some meaning behind the question. "Decimus and I are friends. We share the same Lord."

"Make sure that's all you share," Antonius told her coldly.

Sara placed her hands on her hips in exasperation. "Decimus is like a brother to me!"

Antonius watched her in irritation. She was so truly naive, especially where men were concerned. He felt the anger drain away.

"Sara," he told her gently. "Decimus does not look at you in such a way. Decimus sees you as a woman. The woman he loves."

The color fled from her face and she stared at him in anguish. "No. I don't believe you."

Sighing, Antonius took a step towards her, his lips thinning with displeasure when she backed away. Sara lifted her eyes slowly, encountering the hard blue glare of his penetrating gaze. His eyes captured hers and held her mesmerized against her will.

"Come here, Sara," he commanded gently. Sara shook her head, taking another step backwards. The room was quiet save for the sounds coming from the courtyard below.

Antonius was aggravated that Sara always seemed so frightened of him. Beatrice would have fallen gladly at his feet. Sara, however, always found reasons to avoid his presence. It bothered his ego more than a little bit, though he wouldn't for the world admit it, even to himself.

"Sara." This time there was a definite note of authority in his voice, but Sara refused to move. Antonius realized that she was truly afraid of him. It radiated from every pore in her body, and he realized that he was the cause. Something about him frightened her though he had never laid a hand to her. He frowned in annoyance.

"If I command you to do so, you know you will obey." Antonius wasn't nearly as sure as he sounded. Even from that distance, Antonius could see her body start to tremble. He continued to watch Sara, a well of irritation bubbling up inside him. He could force her, he knew, but what would that accomplish? She would be more frightened of him than ever. Without knowing why, he suddenly turned away.

"Send Decimus to me," he snapped, and Sara bit her bottom lip. Was Decimus to be punished because of her? As she turned away, Antonius called to her softly. She remained motionless, her back facing him.

"You needn't be afraid of me, Sara. I wouldn't harm you."

Her voice came back to him small and still. "Perhaps I am more afraid of myself." With that she quietly departed the room.

Antonius stared after her in surprise. The girl was a definite enigma. Just when he thought he had her figured out, she threw something surprising in his face.

nine

Sara was kneeling in the vegetable garden behind the villa
when Decimus joined her. She glanced up quickly, but
turned away before her eyes had more than a moment to rest
on Decimus' confused face. She had always felt comfortable
around Decimus. Had always felt towards him the way she
would have liked to feel towards Dathan. But in a few short
words, Antonius had destroyed the camaraderie she felt with
Decimus. She was uncomfortable and unsure how to make
matters right. Was it true? Did Decimus love her more than
as a sister, or was it a figment of Antonius' imagination?

Decimus knelt down beside her, tearing ruthlessly at the
weeds in the cucumber patch. His features drew into a frown,
his eyes sparkling with suppressed anger.

"Antonius has forbidden us to mention religious matters to
Diana. He says if he hears of it again he will have us both
flogged."

Sara heaved a sigh of relief. So Antonius hadn't mentioned
their conversation to Decimus. She was able to look at him
more fully, forgetting her own distress in the face of his.

"Did he say why?" she asked softly.

He continued to pull at the weeds and Sara noticed a tear
wend its way down his cheek. Brushing at it impatiently, he
turned towards Sara.

"I would defy him if not for you. I cannot allow him to
punish you." He gritted his teeth fiercely. "But how can I not
talk to Diana when she is so close to accepting the truth!"

Sara laid a hand gently on his arm. "There will be a way.
Remember what the Apostle Paul said. Slaves must obey

their masters. To defy Antonius is to defy God himself."

Releasing a pent up breath, Decimus turned to her and gave her a rather wan smile. "How did you get to be so wise?"

Sara laughed. "I have had a good teacher. The best. My father once heard the apostles speak. It so filled his heart that he has spent the rest of his life trying to share it with others."

Decimus looked at her thoughtfully. "I wonder if my parents have ever heard the salvation message."

"Someday, Decimus, you must take it to them. I believe God has prepared you for just such a message. You have a way about you. People trust you."

He looked hard into her eyes. "Do you trust me?"

Sara reached down to pull a cucumber from the vine even though she could tell it wasn't quite ripe. Her face flooded with embarrassed color. "Of course I do. You are the brother I never had."

He watched her quietly before turning away. "I thought you had a brother."

Relieved to change the subject, Sara told him about Dathan and their life together. He had always been rebellious and selfish, always avoiding work and seeking pleasure wherever he could find it.

Beatrice walked into the garden. "Sara, my lady wants you."

Sara got quickly to her feet, reaching down a hand and squeezing Decimus lightly on the shoulder. "Things will work out. You'll see. Just trust God."

When Sara walked into Diana's room, she could tell that she was extremely upset. A leftover supper tray sat untouched on the table beside her. Diana's hair was mussed and her clothes wrinkled. Sara hadn't seen her look like this in a long while.

"My lady? You wanted me?"

"I'm going crazy up here! Where were you?" Her voice

was almost frenzied, tears shimmering just below the surface of her eyes. It was almost as though they were back to the first step again.

Sara's forehead wrinkled in bewilderment. "I was in the vegetable garden trying to find something special for your meal, but I see Bacchus has already sent it up."

"I don't want anything to eat. Take it away," she commanded imperiously.

Unsure just what had brought about the change, Sara did as she was told. She watched Diana cautiously, hoping that the young girl would confide in her.

"Sara?"

"Yes, my lady?"

"If your God cares so much about you, why does He let bad things happen?" There was a decided anger behind the curiosity.

Sara took a deep breath. Antonius had forbidden her to speak about such things with Diana, and to defy him would be a sin. But wouldn't it be more of a sin to remain silent? The apostle Peter had been forbidden to speak the gospel message, had even been sent to prison when he refused to remain silent. Could she do any less?

"No one knows the mind and ways of God," she told Diana firmly.

"Is that a convenient way of saying you don't know?" she asked sarcastically.

Sara blushed, but her eyes remained unyielding in their intensity. "No, it is just a way of saying I don't always understand. Sometimes things happen that we don't always understand, but eventually they work out for God's purpose."

"Can you give me an instance?"

Thinking hard, Sara finally began to tell Diana the story of Joseph and his rise to power in Egypt. Diana sat enthralled, hanging on every word. When Sara finally finished, Diana looked at her skeptically.

"Is this a true story?"

"Yes, my lady."

"Humph," Diana responded autocratically. "Better to be the slave of a Roman than of an Egyptian."

"Better not to be a slave at all," Sara rejoined softly.

"Tell me another instance," Diana demanded, and Sara began to tell her the story of Queen Esther. Again Diana was captivated by the story. Her eyes became dreamy, a look of such longing in them that Sara was surprised. What was she thinking? Was she remembering her fiancé of time past?

"So God could be using us for His own purposes?"

"It's possible," Sara answered her quietly. "But like I said, I don't know all the answers."

Diana settled back against the cushions, staring off into space. "How can you get God to change someone's mind?"

"What?"

Diana's eyes focused intently on Sara, her eyes filled with purpose. "How can you reach this God of yours?"

Unsure of just what to do, Sara remained absolutely immobile, biting her lip in indecision. She sat down next to Diana and took her small white hand into her own rough brown one.

"Listen to me, Diana. There's a whole lot more to this than you know. Let me try to explain."

For the next hour, Sara urgently related the salvation story to Diana. For some reason she felt that it was imperative to make her understand. They argued back and forth. Diana was reluctant to give up the desire for action on her part. Perhaps if she made a sacrifice to Aphrodite, Flavius would change his mind about his bride and choose Diana instead. She mentioned nothing of this to Sara, and yet Sara sensed more behind the questions than Diana was divulging.

Finally Diana sat back exhausted. "But He's a Jewish God!

What does He care about Romans?"

"He loves everyone, Diana, they just don't know it. He is not a Jewish God. He is not a Jew. He only chose the Jewish people because at that time they had more of a heart for Him. He needed a race of people to bring His son into the world. He chose the Jews, but He could have just as easily chosen someone else. Now that His son has come, He doesn't need to keep a set-apart people. He still loves the Jews, but most of them have rejected the Son He sent to them in love."

Diana shook her head slowly from side to side. "How could they? After all that He did for them?"

"Many of the Jews are still waiting for a warrior king. Someone to help them reclaim what they have lost. They don't understand how great his love is. God is love," Sara finished softly.

When Sara left Diana's room, she still didn't know if Diana truly understood, but Sara felt she had made a step in the right direction. Sara had brushed Diana's hair and helped prepare her for bed. Whatever had been bothering Diana earlier seemed to have been pushed aside for the time being.

❧

Antonius stared around him in aggravation. All the noise and confusion were getting on his nerves, and he longed suddenly for the peace of the villa.

"Don't look now," Flavius interrupted his thoughts, "but the spider has entered and seems to be looking for a particular prey."

All eyes were riveted to the voluptuous redhead threading her way through the throng of people. Antonius had to admit she was well worth looking at, but an image of pure brown eyes suddenly filled his mind. Whatever had made him think of Sara? Shrugging his shoulders, he plastered a smile on his face as Helena stood before him, her emerald green eyes sparkling with intent.

"So, Antonius," she purred. "I haven't seen you in a long while. I've missed you."

Antonius lifted a cynical dark eyebrow. "I find that hard to believe, Helena. The last time you talked to me you assured me I was quite boring."

Color suffused her face and Antonius was impressed. He had assumed Helena had forgotten how to blush a long time ago.

"Only a plebeian would remind me of such a thing," she told him angrily.

Flavius burst into laughter. "And there you have it, Antonius. That should effectively put you in your place."

Helena glared angrily at Flavius. "Why don't you go find someone else to talk to and let Antonius and I exchange apologies."

Flavius pressed his lips tightly together to keep from laughing at Antonius' thunderstruck expression. He got quickly to his feet, patting Antonius on the back. "See you later, old friend."

"I could get you for desertion," Antonius hissed angrily for Flavius' ears alone, which only caused the young man more merriment.

Helena slid down on the cushions next to Antonius, leaning close against his side. She slid one hand suggestively up his arm before latching on to it possessively.

"I hear Diana is much improved. I'm pleased. Now you won't need to run off so often."

Antonius felt the sweat begin to break out on his brow. This party of Gaius' was turning into a show fit for the Circus Maximus. As a soldier, Antonius had faced death many times. Without fear. But this woman clinging to his arm made his mouth go dry with trepidation. How could he have thought her attractive? He must have been blind!

Again Sara's image floated into his mind, and he shook his

head in anger to rid himself of the picture. Sara didn't approve of such parties, and she certainly wouldn't approve of the different people draped over couches in various stages of undress. What she would most disapprove of would be the men with the men and the women with the women. He could almost see her disapproving scowl. Suddenly he felt very unclean. Helena stared at him in surprise when he rose quickly to his feet.

"Excuse me, Helena. There is something I have to do."

"Can't it wait?" she pleaded. "We could go to my house if you have had enough of the crowd." Her voice lowered suggestively. "I could help you relax."

Swallowing hard, Antonius shook his head. "Perhaps I will see you again," he told her dismissively and knew he would feel her wrath sooner or later. He headed quickly for the exit, not breathing until he reached the outside. He released his breath slowly, feeling as though he had just barely managed to escape with his life.

The afternoon sun warmed his face as he lifted it to the sky, dragging in deep clean breaths. Flavius followed him out the door. "Is it just me, or have these parties begun to pall?"

Antonius looked at him wryly. "You didn't have to leave on my account."

"Why not?" Flavius wanted to know. "I only went on your account."

Antonius grinned. "Well, do me a favor the next time I'm tempted to go. Remind me that I might run into Helena."

Flavius shivered melodramatically. "The gods forbid!"

As they walked out the gate, Antonius turned to his friend solemnly. "What's happening to us, Flavius? All of a sudden I seem to be on the outside looking in."

Nodding his head in agreement, Flavius smiled at his friend. "Maybe we're just getting old."

Antonius blew through his lips. "Speak for yourself, old man." He shook his head. "No, it's more than that. I find myself condemning things I used to participate in. The parties are only a part of it."

"Perhaps you've had your head in those dusty old manuscripts too much lately."

"Then what's your excuse?"

Flavius grinned wryly, but shook his head. Antonius stared at him, a sudden illumination lighting up his eyes. "A woman!"

Color raced up Flavius' neck, spreading across his face and into his hairline. Antonius laughed aloud, drawing the attention of several passersby. "As I live and breathe! Why didn't you mention it to me? Who is she?"

Before Flavius had time to answer, Antonius placed a hand on his arm. Looking at Antonius, Flavius found Antonius' eyes focused elsewhere, a frown on his face. Following the direction of his gaze, Flavius noticed Sara hurrying along on the other side of the street. She was deep in conversation with the boy at her side. When she broke into laughter, Flavius noticed the thunderclouds forming in Antonius' eyes.

Flavius' eyebrows flew upwards as he watched the little drama unfolding before him. A sudden suspicion caused him to narrow his eyes and follow Sara's movements more carefully. Surely not. Antonius in love with a slave? And the girl wasn't even pretty. There had to be another explanation, but what he saw in Antonius' eyes he had seen before in others. Stark jealousy.

"I have something to do," Antonius told him absently. "I'll talk to you later."

Flavius watched Antonius cross the street and head in the direction the pair had disappeared. Shaking his head, he turned in the opposite direction. At least Antonius had been sidetracked from further questioning him about the woman in his life. How could he tell Antonius that the woman was his own sister? Antonius believed that they had a brother/sister relationship. Flavius shook his head. There was nothing brotherly about the way he felt for Diana. Someday he would have to face Antonius with a declaration of his love for Diana, but at least the time had been postponed. He sighed with relief.

❧

Antonius followed Sara and Decimus through several alleyways and past the marketplace. He had assumed they were going to the market, but their basket was full of goods and they were going in the opposite direction from the villa. His thoughts heavy with suspicion, he stayed close without being seen.

Antonius stopped when they stopped. Decimus put his hands on Sara's shoulders, his face intent on what he had to say. Sara seemed to be arguing with him, and Decimus finally nodded his head in resignation. When Sara would have passed him to enter the dirty apartment, he reached out a hand and stopped her. Bending down, he kissed her cheek, and Antonius felt the pain in his jaws from clenching his teeth together.

When Sara had gone inside, Decimus stood watch at the door. Antonius watched until the sun started to descend before Sara returned. When she came outside, Antonius noticed that her basket was empty. He frowned, trying to assess the situation. Something was going on here and it definitely didn't make sense.

Antonius ducked into an open doorway when they came his way, their heads close together as they discussed something. He stayed hidden until they were far enough ahead of him for him to feel comfortable with the fact that they didn't suspect they had been followed. Drifting along the streets in their wake, he followed them back to the villa.

❧

Sara was in the peristyle gathering flowers for Diana's room when she looked up and found Antonius watching her. The blue of his eyes was almost hidden by the black of his pupils, his face cast in granite. He stood so until Sara began to feel uneasy with his perusal.

"You wanted something, Tribune?" she asked him uncertainly.

"Where were you today?" he demanded coldly, and Sara could feel a knot forming in the pit of her stomach.

"I. . .I went to the market."

"Alone?"

Flushing, she looked down at the flowers in her arms. "No. Decimus was with me."

Antonius came to stand before her. She could feel the rage vibrating from his body. She sensed his unleashed violence and began to tremble.

"You went only to the market?" he insisted, his voice tinged with frost.

Sara bit her lip, wondering where these questions were leading. Had Antonius somehow found out about her and Decimus? And if so, how? She pulled in her breath, trying to relax. They had done nothing wrong. Not really.

"Answer me, Sara. Or should I call Decimus?"

Sara's head flew up, and Antonius' lips pressed together at the fear he saw there.

"You don't need to call. I am here." Both Sara and Antonius turned to watch as Decimus came through the back garden entrance. He walked purposefully, coming to stand beside Sara. His eyes lifted defiantly to Antonius.

"What were the two of you doing at the market?" Antonius bit out savagely.

"Shopping," Decimus told him calmly.

Quick as a flash of lightning, Antonius had the boy by the front of his tunic, lifting him clear of the ground. Sara screamed, trying to pry them apart. Antonius' eyes glittered with rage, and Sara feared for Decimus' life.

"Tribune! Please!"

"What's going on here?"

Antonius dropped Decimus to the ground, where the boy began rubbing his throat. Sara bent to him, but her eyes were raised upwards in astonishment. Antonius stood transfixed, his eyes locked onto his sister, who was leaning against the balcony with all her strength. In a moment Antonius was up the stairs, lifting her gently into his arms.

"What do you think you're doing?" he demanded fiercely.

"I heard Sara scream. What's happening? What were you doing to Decimus!" Diana's voice rose higher and higher.

"Shhh," Antonius begged. "You'll upset yourself."

"I'm already upset," she told him. "I want to know what you were doing."

Antonius' eyes flashed downward to where Sara was still leaning over Decimus. Both of them were staring in horror up at Antonius, who was feeling more than a little foolish at the moment. He hadn't even given them time to explain.

"Both of you come up here. Now!"

Sara helped Decimus get to his feet, and Antonius watched as they began to ascend the stairs. They looked like a pair about to face the execution squad. Antonius smiled grimly. No, he hadn't given them a chance to explain, but he would now. And it had better be one good explanation.

ten

"A Christian! Are you out of your mind?" The thunder of Antonius' wrathful voice echoed throughout the room.

Diana sighed. "Sit down, Antonius, and stop roaring at me like a lion! Let me explain."

Antonius whirled on Decimus. "This is your doing! By the gods, I should have the skin stripped from your back."

Decimus remained still, the only outward show of emotion the paling of his face.

Sara opened her mouth to speak, but Diana interrupted angrily. "You'll do no such thing! Decimus had nothing to do with this."

Antonius fixed his eyes on Sara, their hard glitter giving evidence of the rage he had worked himself into. "Then it must be your doing."

Again Diana intervened. "It was not Sara's doing nor was it Decimus'. It was my own decision. You cannot blame them for answering the questions I asked of them."

"Can't I?" Antonius' voice was more frightening in its quietness than his previous ranting. His eyes glowed almost obsidian, and Sara felt herself swallow in fear. "I seem to remember commanding them not to speak of religious things to you."

Diana tried to rise from the couch, leaning heavily on the table next to it. Antonius became instantly alarmed and went to her, trying to get her to settle back down again.

"If you won't sit down, then I'll stand up," she told him firmly.

"All right! All right, I'll sit down," he relented, and Diana collapsed back with a sigh of relief.

"Decimus, you and Sara may leave," she told them.

"No!" Antonius was back on his feet in an instant.

"Antonius," Diana pleaded. "I would rather speak with you about this alone."

Staring down at her, Antonius felt some of the anger drain away. Whatever had happened, Diana was much like the girl she used to be. A sparkle in her eyes gave evidence of the life that again flourished within her. She had almost died, and now here she was vibrant and full of purpose. And she had walked. Praise the gods. Or should he thank Sara's unseen God?

"Go," he told them without taking his eyes from his sister. "Decimus, you will wait for me in the bibliotheca."

Sara and Decimus exchanged glances. "As you wish, my lord."

When they had gone, Antonius turned back to his sister. "You have a lot of explaining to do. And what is this about you becoming a Christian? It's. . .it's preposterous. I forbid it, Diana!"

"Antonius," she told him softly. "You can't forbid me to believe what I believe. As the head of our family you have the right to forbid me many things, and command me to do others, but you cannot control what's in my mind. Nor in my heart."

What she said was true, and Antonius felt the anger returning as he felt his own helplessness. He needed to be calm if he wished to sway Diana from this way of thinking. She could be as stubborn as he was at times. Taking a deep breath, he sat down beside her, taking her hand into his own.

Diana reached up with her other hand and laid it against his cheek. "Before you say anything, let me tell you something. I didn't just believe overnight. I've given this a lot of thought. I've had enough time, that's for sure. I started asking questions, I guess, years ago. Maybe when Decimus first became a Christian himself. We talked about it a lot."

She slid her hand down, wrapping it around his hand with her other. "Decimus is not a Jew."

"I'm aware of that," he told her irritably.

"But he accepted a Jewish God. That intrigued me. We spoke of it often. Then Sara came to us, and. . .well, you know what happened. I owe her my life."

Antonius jerked to his feet, pacing the floor like a caged lion. He pushed his hands through his hair, dropping them helplessly to his sides. "She has filled your mind with all kinds of nonsense."

"No, Antonius. She has not. She only answered the questions I asked of her. I figured this out for myself."

For the first time, Antonius noticed a difference about his sister. She looked more mature, more in tune with her emotions. He was suddenly filled with foreboding. He had no idea what this change meant for their lives.

"What have you figured out?" he asked her quietly.

"That of all the gods and goddesses, of all the religions, of all the beliefs, this one makes sense."

Antonius went and sat down by her side again. Sighing, he looked deeply into her eyes to see if he could read the truth there. "How does it make sense that a God who loved His people would treat them the way He has? Their race has been almost completely destroyed."

"Antonius, do you remember the time you and Father disagreed about the way you should live your life? You wanted to join the legion, and he wanted you to take over his business enterprises."

"I remember," Antonius told her grimly, thinking back to that time that had caused the first real breach in their father/son relationship. He had wanted to please his father, but he had wanted to please himself more. In the end,

Antonius had his way, but it had left a sour taste in his mouth.

"He could have commanded you, but that would only have driven you farther away. God is like that."

"Diana. . ."

"Wait. I'm not finished. Romans believe that the Christian religion is abhorrent. Detestable. But what could be so wrong about a faith that teaches you to love everyone, even your enemies? Imagine if everyone embraced this philosophy."

Antonius turned to her in anger. "Not everyone will. It's impossible."

"With God, all things are possible, but you're probably right. That's not what I'm asking. What if I were? What is so bad about such a thing?"

Antonius began massaging his forehead with his hands. "This religion preaches anarchy."

"Rubbish! How can this be so when the Scriptures teach that a slave should obey his master?"

His head snapped up and he glared at her. "If this were so, why did Sara disobey me and continue to fill your head with such foolish notions?"

Diana smiled. "Fortunately for me, Sara has a different master."

"So I've heard," Antonius returned dryly.

"Jesus taught His followers to obey the laws of the land, as long as they didn't conflict with God's own laws."

"I can't believe you've fallen for this!"

Diana pressed her lips grimly together. "All right, Antonius. I'll make you a challenge. Find some of the old scrolls of the Jewish prophets. Read them. Study them. Use your mind. Then. . .then your heart will follow."

Antonius decided that he was getting nowhere. Maybe she was right. If he could find something in the Jewish scriptures to convince her, she might be more reasonable.

"All right," he told her. "I'll do that, but in the meantime I want you to keep this quiet. Romans have always hated Jews, and the winds stirring among the people are not favorable to them. I command you to be silent about this. Worship this Jewish God if it brings you pleasure, but do it quietly."

"Whatever happened to Roman tolerance of all religions? Is Rome so afraid of the truth?"

Antonius decided to ignore her. "As for this other matter, I will not have you giving away our food to all the riff raff of this city."

"But. . ."

Getting to his feet, Antonius went to the door and threw it open. "Sara!" He bellowed.

Sara must have been in the peristyle below, because she came rapidly to his side. "Yes, Tribune?"

"Come in. I want you to hear what I have to say."

Sara followed him inside, glancing with trepidation at Diana's tense face. He closed the door and leaned his back against it.

"I was just telling my sister that I refuse to feed the entire poor population of this city."

"You called them riff raff, I believe," Diana answered him sarcastically. "Would you consider General Titus to be such?"

Antonius frowned. "What are you talking about?"

"Do you remember General Titus, Antonius?" she asked him quietly.

"Of course I do. My first command was under him. What does he have to do with this?"

"He's one of the riff raff I've been helping."

"That's not possible! He's a retired general. Rome takes care of its own."

"Not when they're Christians," Diana told him quietly, and watched the color leave his face. A hurt look came into his eyes and Sara felt pity for him, but she realized he would not appreciate her concern. She dropped her lashes to hide her feelings.

Diana got slowly to her feet, holding up her hand imperiously when Antonius and Sara would have rushed to her assistance. She walked slowly, falteringly, across the space to her brother's side. Touching his arm gently, she lowered her voice placatingly. "Please, Antonius. We have so much. You are willing to give food to marble idols, why not to living people?"

Antonius stared at her for what seemed an eternity. Sara was not aware she was holding her breath until Antonius sighed, laying his palm gently against Diana's cheek.

"Very well," he told her and a bright smile broke across Diana's face, only to vanish a moment later when he continued. "But you will not deliver the goods yourself, and I will not have Sara wandering around that section of the city. Send Trophus."

"But. . ."

"I forbid it, Diana." For all its quietness, steel threaded his voice.

Diana set her lips mutinously, giving back glare for glare. It was easy to see the resemblance between brother and sister when they stood thus. Reaching down, Antonius lifted Diana into his arms and carried her back to her couch. Straightening, he stroked a hand down her cheek and turned and walked out of the room.

≈

Antonius entered the bibliotheca where Decimus stood staring out the window. The boy turned at his entrance, his eyes veiled. Clearing his throat, Antonius reached for a scroll that was on his desk. Curling it, he then placed it carefully in a case and held it out to the boy.

Decimus stared suspiciously at the container, one eyebrow ascending to his blonde hair. "You wish me to deliver this, my lord?" he asked, reaching slowly for the scroll.

"It's yours," Antonius told him shortly. "Your freedom papers."

Decimus jerked his hand away, his eyes opening wide. "You are giving me my freedom?" he asked, suddenly suspicious. "Why?"

Antonius frowned in annoyance. "That's a stupid question to ask. Take the scroll."

"Not so stupid, my lord," he replied quietly. "Why now?"

"I want you away from Diana. I don't want her head filled with your heathenish religion."

Decimus shook his head slowly. "You had that scroll prepared before you found out about Diana's commitment to Christianity."

Antonius felt rage begin to bubble inside at the familiar use of Diana's name. Taking a breath, he tried to regain control.

"Think carefully, Decimus," he gritted. "I am offering you your freedom. You can return to your people. Your country. I had it in mind to send you away with enough money to help you get started in your new life. You have served this family well."

"And if I don't wish to leave?"

The quietly spoken question caused Antonius' eyes to darken, his face becoming a hard mask.

"You will not stay here," he told him ominously. "You can leave here a free man, or you can leave here a slave, but you will leave."

Decimus bit his lip in indecision. Antonius was in a towering rage, that was all too clear. Maybe when he calmed down he would regret this action, but the Lord only knew when, or if, that might be.

"And what of Sara?" he dared to ask.

Flames ignited in Antonius' eyes and Decimus took a step backward, though Antonius himself had not moved.

"Sara has nothing to do with you."

"I love her," Decimus told him quietly. "I cannot leave her here. I want to marry her."

Decimus sensed more than saw Antonius' rising anger. He thought he understood and that understanding gave him the strength to continue. "She is a Christian, too," he told Antonius reasonably. "Surely you don't want her around Diana."

"Don't push me, Decimus."

Swallowing hard, Decimus decided he might as well go all the way. He had nothing to lose. "May I speak to Sara?"

A muscle worked convulsively in Antonius' jaw. Decimus thought for sure that Antonius was going to refuse his request. Instead, an unusual calm seemed to settle around him. "Go ahead, but Sara will remain here. Make sure you make that clear to her."

Decimus found Sara in the peristyle, staring up at the risen crescent moon. Stars filled the dark expanse of the sky. Torches were lit in the garden, and though he could not see her face clearly, he could tell she was smiling.

"What makes you so happy?" he asked her softly. "What are you thinking about?"

She jumped slightly, turning her head quickly in his direction. "You startled me," she told him breathlessly, a smile returning to her face. "I was just thinking how God works in such mysterious ways."

Decimus sat down beside her. He pulled a hibiscus blossom from its bush and placed it gently in Sara's hair. She frowned at him uncertainly.

"What bothers you, Decimus? I see worry in your eyes."

He looked away from her, trying to gather his scattered thoughts. "Sara, Antonius has given me my freedom."

Sara's eyes went wide in shock, the color draining from her face. Her eyes flew swiftly around the peristyle before returning to rest on Decimus' face. Suddenly her face came alive with joy.

"But Decimus, this is wonderful! Now you can go home to your people. You can tell them about God."

Sighing, he buried his face in his hands. "It's not that simple."

Totally confused, Sara placed a hand gently on his downbent head. "I don't understand."

Brushing his hands back through his hair, he lifted his head and stared intently into her eyes. "I won't leave you. I told him I want to marry you."

Sara sat back in stunned amazement. She couldn't think of a thing to say. It had never occurred to her that Antonius might be right in his assessment of Decimus' feelings. She had thought it a case of mistaken imagination on Antonius' part.

"What did he say?" she asked softly, suddenly fearful of what might be coming. She had no desire to leave. She loved Decimus, but not like he wanted.

"He said to make clear to you that you cannot leave." Decimus gritted his teeth in impotent anger. He had been trying to think of a way, but he kept coming to the same conclusion. Either he left a free man or he would leave sold to someone else. The pain of it caused tears to come to his eyes. He turned away from Sara, not wanting her to see.

Sara watched him thoughtfully. She could sense Decimus' pain, but she could not help her own relief. She never meant to hurt Decimus, and though she didn't take his feelings lightly, neither did she believe him in love with her to the extent that he seemed to feel.

"I cannot marry you, Decimus," she told him softly, trying to shield him from more pain. "I don't love you the way you mean. Not the way my parents love each other." His shoulders slumped in defeat, and Sara felt torn. Stroking his back in slow moving circles with her hand, she began to reason with him. "I told you God had a purpose for you. I told you that one day you would go home and spread God's word. Now that time has come."

A tear slid down Decimus' cheek, and Sara gently wiped it away. "Someday, you will meet the woman God meant for you to marry, and you will be glad you waited."

He shook his head vehemently. "Never!"

Sara hid a smile. He sounded so much like a hurt child.

Suddenly he turned to her, his eyes alive with hope. "I could ask Diana to release you also."

"Antonius has the final say in this family. What would he say?" Sara was unsure just why Antonius refused to let her go with Decimus, and she was unsure why it made her feel excited inside that he was so unwilling to let her go, but she thought his reasoning probably had something to do with Diana.

Decimus turned away. "You want me to go?"

"Oh, Decimus! Part of me will cry for your loss, but the other part of me thrills for your release." She took his face between her palms and smiled gently into his eyes. "Go with God. And don't forget your little Jewish sister."

Decimus gave a halfhearted attempt at a smile. "I could never forget you." Turning away, he sighed and got to his feet. "I'll tell Antonius that I accept his offer."

Sara watched him walk with bowed head from the garden, and her heart ached for him. It occurred to her that she knew just what it was like to love someone who didn't love you back.

❧

Decimus took the scroll from Antonius. He watched him silently. Using his newfound freedom, he decided to say what needed to be said. "Sara is a very special woman. I hope that she will never be hurt."

Antonius recognized the threat in Decimus' voice, but surprisingly he felt no offense. "I have no intention of hurting her," he told him quietly.

Nodding his head, Decimus began to twirl the scroll in his hands. "May I say goodbye to Diana?"

Again Antonius took offense at the use of her name. Then it suddenly occurred to him that Decimus and Diana had been more than slave and master. They had been friends. Would Sara ever get over her fear of him and feel that way, too? He nodded his permission. Reaching his hand into the gold box on his desk, he pulled out a small bag of money. He handed it to Decimus, who did nothing towards taking it.

"Please," Antonius told him. "For Diana. She would be very distressed if she knew you wouldn't take it. You deserve it."

Slowly Decimus took the bag, clenching it in his hand. He stared at Antonius a long moment before he turned and walked out of the room.

eleven

Over the next several weeks, Antonius found himself watching Sara more and more. He looked for her whenever he entered the villa and found himself disappointed if she were not around. He began to call her to him in the bibliotheca, supposedly to discuss some of the Jewish writings he had managed to buy.

At first, Sara was reluctant. But as Antonius shared the writings on his scrolls with her, she began to relax and look forward to those times. As a child, her father had read from the old scrolls, but Sara had been too little at the time to remember much. Now she found herself fascinated by the writings of the old prophets.

Antonius would watch her eyes light when he read particular passages, and he would wonder what had caused her response. She would patiently answer his questions, but he could tell she was holding herself back for some reason.

Sara began to explain to him the meanings behind the prophecies and their fulfillment in the man called Jesus Christ. It still made no sense to him that a god would allow His son to be crucified on a cross, the cruelest, most detestable form of punishment there was. Any argument he had, though, was met with reasoning and logic from Sara. She had an answer for everything. It amazed him that a woman could speak so intelligently.

On this particular day, they were lightly arguing about the attributes of deities.

"If this Jesus was a god, how could He have died?" Antonius wanted to know.

"It was because He was God that He had to find a way to live as a man. He allowed a part of Himself to become mixed with a human so that He might better understand us. Our temptations, our desires. There was nothing He didn't experience. But because He was God, when the time came for His mortal body to die, He was still able to overcome death."

Sara frowned at his cynical smile and decided to try again. "Romans claim that the emperor is a god, is this not so?"

"That is so," Antonius agreed.

"And yet Augustus, Tiberius and Caligula are all dead. And some day Claudius will die also. If he were a god, he wouldn't need the food tasters and the bodyguards."

Antonius would have argued, but he couldn't. She was right. But how did that make her God any different then? He had died also.

"I know what you're thinking," she told him softly. "But there is a difference. Jesus allowed Himself to die so that we might live. He died, but He arose again. He overcame death. Over five hundred people witnessed this."

Surprised that she could read his mind so well, Antonius turned away and looked out the window. He had been reading some of the Jewish prophecies that had predicted the downfall of the Jewish people. Some of the conquerors were predicted by name over a hundred years before that king was ever born. It was uncanny.

He had spoken with some of the soldiers who had been in Jerusalem when the man Jesus had been crucified. The stories they told him made his blood run cold. Since Antonius himself had only been ten at the time, he didn't remember very much about the man that had caused such an uproar in the Roman republic.

One of the centurions that had been in Jerusalem at the time, and had served Pontius Pilate, was himself now a

Christian. What kind of attraction could this religion have that so many people would flock to it even in the face of persecution? The thing that upset Romans so much was the fact that it taught equality for everyone.

"May I go now, Tribune?" Sara's soft voice interrupted his thoughts. "It is almost time for lunch, and Diana wanted to have it in the peristyle."

He nodded his head and watched her walk gracefully towards the door. "Wait!"

She stopped and looked at him inquiringly. "Yes, Tribune?"

He crossed the space to her and stood looking down into her expressive eyes. "Do you still miss Decimus?" he asked her quietly and studied her face intently.

She dropped her eyes, but he lifted her face by cupping her chin in his large, rough palm.

"Do you?" he wanted to know.

"Very much," she told him truthfully. She had longed for her friend to confide in many times. She missed his company when preparing baskets of food for those that Diana chose to help. She missed his laughter that so many times helped her over her own periods of depression. And if she were not mistaken, Diana missed him just as much.

Antonius rubbed his thumb gently over Sara's lips and saw the fear return to her eyes. Was she so afraid of him, or was she, as she had said, afraid of herself? He decided to find out.

He lowered his mouth to hers, holding her firmly when she would have moved away. When his lips met hers, he let out an unconscious sigh. This is what he had longed to do for some time now.

Sara tried to hold herself rigid beneath the onslaught to her senses. Her mind clouded and reason seemed to be slipping away. When Antonius wrapped his arms around her, she found herself leaning into his kiss, returning it with a fervor she didn't know she possessed.

Antonius was surprised at Sara's capitulation. Feelings he had never felt before swirled through his body, capturing his mind and his heart. Suddenly he longed for something more. He realized that what he felt for Sara transcended the physical, causing him to yearn for things he hadn't known existed. But what it was, he wasn't quite sure. These feelings were new to him.

He lifted his lips from Sara's and slowly dropped his arms to his side. Feeling him withdrawing, Sara came back to her senses. She looked into Antonius' eyes and saw the veil that descended over them to hide his thoughts. Face flooding with color at her forwardness, she turned and fled.

❧

"Antonius, I would speak to you about something."

Antonius grinned at his friend, pulling Orion to a stop. Flavius reined in his mount also and sat chewing on his lip. For the last several miles Flavius had been utterly preoccupied. Antonius had wondered if he would share what was troubling him or if he would keep it to himself.

"Well?" Antonius encouraged.

Flavius' eyes scanned the horizon in every direction, refusing to meet Antonius' eyes, that were beginning to fill with suspicion.

"Is it about this unknown girl you refuse to share with me?"

Color flooded Flavius' face, and he felt his heart pound with trepidation. "You already know her," he told Antonius quietly.

Antonius stared at his friend, his mind trying to figure out the person to whom Flavius was referring. Obviously, Flavius feared his wrath. Suddenly his eyes widened and he turned on Flavius. "Not Helena!"

Flavius glared at him. "By the gods, Antonius. Give me

credit for having some sense."

Antonius looked perplexed then. "For the love of Poseidon, tell me then."

Gaining his composure, Flavius lifted his chin firmly, staring boldly at Antonius. "I am referring to Diana."

Antonius felt his mind go blank with incredulity. His sister? His little Diana? She was but a child! He felt his anger begin to rise and as suddenly dissipate. Sara was as old as Diana, and hadn't he been seeing her in much the same way?

"How long has this been going on?" Antonius asked him angrily.

Flavius frowned. "There's nothing going on."

"Then what are you talking about?"

Sighing, Flavius dismounted and began walking towards a little copse of trees. "If we're going to discuss this, let's do it in the shade."

Dismounting also, Antonius followed Flavius and joined him where he sat on a fallen tree. He realized that Flavius looked as though he were about to face a gladiator and not his best friend.

Antonius sighed. "Let's hear it, Flavius."

"I love Diana, Antonius. I have for a long time." He swallowed hard before continuing. "When I thought she was going to die. . .I thought I would die also," he finished quietly.

Antonius could well understand his feelings. Leaning his elbow on his knee and putting his cheek in his palm, Antonius turned to Flavius.

"So just what exactly are you saying, Flavius? You momentarily caught me off guard, but I am rational now." He smiled wryly, and Flavius returned his smile.

"I want to marry her."

Something flickered briefly in Antonius' eyes. "Have you spoken of this to her?"

"Once," he answered softly, and Antonius wondered at the

pain in his voice. He sat up straight.

"And did she reject you?"

"Not exactly."

Antonius became exasperated. "Well, speak up, man. What did she say?"

Flavius picked up a stick from the ground and began to break it into little pieces. His forehead creased in a frown. "She said she would never marry. That she couldn't leave you."

Surprised, Antonius stared hard at his friend. "She told you this? Did she tell you that she didn't love you?"

Flavius shook his head. "No. We didn't speak of love."

"What? You aren't making sense, Flavius."

"The last time I came to your house I told Diana I was resigning my commission so that I could get married."

Sudden understanding caused a grin to spread across Antonius' face. "I assume you didn't say to whom you wished to get married?"

Frowning at him, Flavius pressed his lips together. "How could I?" Turning away, he lowered his head and dropped the pieces of stick to the ground. "She didn't give me a chance," he finished lamely.

Antonius laughed, pounding Flavius on the back. "I think maybe you two were at cross purposes, my friend. I'm not sure if Diana loves you in the same way, but I think she might."

Flavius glanced up quickly, hope filling his eyes. "You truly think so? And this would be all right with you?"

Antonius answered him softly. "I can think of no one that I would rather have for a brother. Come to dinner tonight, and maybe together we can convince my sister of this also."

"It must be her decision," Flavius warned.

"Agreed."

"I can't marry you, Flavius." Diana stood trembling between her brother and Flavius, tears shimmering in her eyes.

"What?"

"Antonius." Flavius' warning stopped Antonius in his tracks. His fists curled at his sides. What was going through his sister's mind now? He had seen her eyes fill with joy when Flavius spoke of his love, then the joy had faded and turned to sorrow. One thing he was convinced of. Diana loved Flavius as much as he loved her.

"I don't understand," Flavius told Diana softly. "Do you not love me?"

Diana struggled with an answer that wouldn't bring down the wrath of her already sensitive brother. That Flavius loved her was more than she had ever dared to hope. Weeks ago she would have flown into his arms at such a declaration of love as he had given her. But now she was a child of Christ. If she told him so she knew his eyes would fill with loathing. But she would not deny her Lord. He had made a remarkable change in her life already. Believing she had lost Flavius to another, she had found solace in the peace that Jesus had brought to her life. Although she had hurt, she hadn't hurt nearly as badly as she would have before she found Him. She couldn't turn her back on Him now.

Flavius came to Diana, lifting her bowed head. He looked seriously into her misty blue eyes. "If you tell me you don't love me, I will never mention this again. But I would always like to remain your friend."

The simple words that would leave her life intact refused to be said. She couldn't deny her Lord, but neither could she lie and deny her love for this wonderful man.

"I love you, Flavius," she told him tenderly, and watched the joy that filled his face. "But I can't marry you."

"I don't understand," he frowned in confusion. "Is it because of Antonius? Because he has already agreed."

Diana looked at her brother and knew that her answer would displease him. He had such a volatile temper, and she knew she was about to light the fire within him. "I can't because I'm a Christian," she told Flavius, though her eyes never left her brother.

Flavius stared at her, dumbfounded. "By the gods!" he whispered, suddenly dropping to the couch behind him.

No one spoke, and the eerie silence became oppressive. Finally, Flavius brushed his hand through his dark hair, lifting his eyes to stare broodingly at Diana. He seemed to suddenly come to a decision. Getting up, he went to Diana and took her by the shoulders. She dropped her eyes in embarrassment, not able to see the loathing she felt sure would be there.

"Look at me, Diana," he commanded gently and she raised her eyes slowly to his. His brown eyes were aglow with his love, and Diana caught her breath. "I don't care what religion you choose, or what god you choose to worship. I want to marry you anyway."

Diana felt her heart beat rapidly in response to his words, and tears came to her eyes. He still loved her, even though she admitted her Christianity. If she married him, could she win him to her Lord? Could she, by example, show him the true way? And if he never believed, what then? Would it make a difference? Couldn't two people who truly loved each other live together in harmony even though they had different beliefs? *No, they couldn't*, her mind told her, and realized that Satan was giving her a full taste of his power. How easy it would be to give in.

"I can't marry you, Flavius. I can't." Diana pushed his hands away and fled the room, Sara close on her heels.

Flavius stared at Antonius uncomprehendingly. "I don't understand."

"I think I do," Antonius told him grimly. "These Christians are as zealous in their beliefs as are the Jews. When they believe something, they hold to it fiercely."

"But Diana. . ." Flavius shook his head in confusion.

"Listen to me, Flavius," Antonius muttered. "Diana has been corrupted by these Christians. She needs to be gotten away from their influence."

Flavius glared at him. "Isn't Sara a Christian also?"

Antonius drew up his shoulders, his face becoming a bland mask. "Leave Sara to me."

"But what can I do? You heard her say she wouldn't marry me!"

"She will if I decide it," Antonius answered firmly.

Flavius watched the feelings chasing themselves across Antonius' face. He shook his head. "I can't force her, Antonius. She would only hate me in the end."

"I don't think so. You heard her say she loves you."

"She loves me now, but what of later?"

"If you can get her to forget this Christianity business, there will be no problem."

Flavius sighed. "And if I can't?"

Antonius smiled wryly. "I have faith in you, my friend."

Flavius lifted an apple from the supper tray, turning it slowly around in his fingers, Putting it back, he turned to Antonius. "Very well. What do we do?"

"Leave the arrangements to me." Antonius clanged the bronze gong sitting on the table, and Beatrice entered the room. "Send Sara to me," he told her.

Sara came moments later, the thin blue material of her tunic drifting around her. Her sandals clicked across the marble floor as she came to stand before him. Lowering her eyes respectfully, she inquired, "Yes, Tribune?"

"Sara, I am sending you to your parents for awhile."

Her eyes flew up in surprise and Antonius felt himself drawn into their deep brown depths. "You will go tomorrow and return in a fortnight."

She gave him a puzzled look, but quickly lowered her eyes. She was filled with apprehension, wondering what Antonius was up to now. She knew it had something to do with Diana and Flavius, and she was reluctant to leave, but she had no choice. And it would be good to stay with her parents for awhile.

"Yes, Tribune. I will make ready," she told him softly.

It suddenly occurred to Antonius that Sara would be gone, and he would not see her for awhile. He missed her when she was gone for a few hours. What would it be like when she was gone for two weeks? Maybe during that two weeks he could rid himself of his obsession with her. Whatever happened, things would be changed when she returned.

twelve

Sara touched the mezuzah slanted on the doorpost that contained the sacred writings of the Shema and thought about the words it contained. "Hear O Israel: the Lord our God is one Lord: And thou shalt love the Lord thy God with all thine heart, and with all thy soul, and with all thy might."

She spread her fingers softly against the mezuzah and wondered if that was possible for her now, because no matter how hard she tried to deny it, she knew that Antonius held a large portion of her heart.

He was coming for her today, and her heart was already responding just thinking about it. She remembered his soft kiss and how she had unashamedly responded to it. Color mounted to her cheeks. She must forget. He was a heathen who worshipped stone idols. Why had God let this happen to her? Why couldn't she have loved Decimus instead?

Entering the house, she found her mother singing in the kitchen. Sara smiled. For as long as she could remember, she had enjoyed the sound of her mother's lilting voice going about her daily duties. She laid the water bag on the table.

"Did you hear any news at the well today?" her mother asked curiously.

Sara thought about the reaction of the villagers, many of them her friends. They were suspicious of her, and with good reason. They couldn't understand how she could be happy serving a Roman. Frankly, she couldn't understand it herself. She should be miserable and yet she longed to return.

"Hannah is getting married," she told her mother, picking up a knife and helping her remove the seeds from the dates.

Her mother looked surprised. "To whom?"

"Daniel Barjamin."

"Jamin's son? Little Daniel?" Abigail shook her head. "It seems that our children marry younger and younger."

Sara grinned. "Mother, you know that you were only fifteen when you married father."

"And how old is Hannah?"

"The same age as I am," she returned with humor.

Abigail again shook her head. "Seventeen. How is it possible? The time has flown so quickly. You need to think of marrying soon yourself."

The smile left Sara's face. "I am a slave, mother. Had you forgotten?"

Abigail looked stricken. "I'm sorry, Sara. It's been so much like old times that I had forgotten." Her face became solemn with her thoughts.

Regretting her sharp words, Sara hugged her mother. "Let's not think of it right now."

Her mother looked sad for a moment. "But you have to go back today."

Sara decided to change the subject. "Father is finished with Ahaz's sickle. I thought I might return it to him."

"I'm sure your father would appreciate it."

Laying down the knife, Sara went through the connecting door to her father's shop. She found him bent over the forge, sweat pouring down his bare back. At fifty years of age, her father still had an athlete's build. No doubt from working the forge day in and day out.

She laid her hands on his shoulders and began to briskly massage his muscles.

"I have missed your touch," he told her. "Your mother is far too gentle."

Sara laughed. "Don't let her hear you say that."

Her father smiled wryly. "That's for sure. She'd probably

strip the skin from my hide the next time."

"I thought I'd take Ahaz his sickle," Sara told him.

"Good idea. He's too old to come for it, and I'm too busy to bring it to him. Besides, I'm sure he'd like to visit with you."

Sara grinned. "I'll be back before long."

Taking the sickle, Sara started walking down the street, heading for Ahaz's house. She smiled as she thought of the old man. He had always been like an uncle to her, complaining that she was always under his feet. From the time she had been able to walk, she could remember being fascinated by Ahaz and his potions and mixtures.

She tapped at his door, touching the mezuzah before she went inside. "Shalom," she told him.

"Shalom, Sara," he grinned back. "What brings you to see an old man?"

"I brought you your sickle."

"Ah. Then bring it in and have a seat."

Sara joined him at his table, sitting on the mat provided. Although the structure was crumbling, it was clean inside.

"So, tell me of Ephesus," he commanded softly.

Sara shook her head slightly. "So many idols. So many unhappy people. They look for hope in their marble statues and find only emptiness."

"And what of you, Sara?" he asked. "What have you found?"

Color filled her face, and she dropped her eyes to the floor. "I have found many friends. Many of them belonging to The Way."

Ahaz nodded his head wisely. Sara knew that he could probably tell more from what she didn't say, than from what she did. He got to his feet and ambled slowly to the door, peering up into the hills.

"What are you looking for?" Sara asked him.

"Nopet hasn't yet returned."

Sara hid a smile. The old man's love for his ewe was well-known by all the villagers. Everyone kept an eye on her, knowing how lost the old man would be without her. Nopet. Honey from a honeycomb, he called her. His pride and joy.

"Would you like me to go look for her?" she asked.

He watched the sun starting to descend from its zenith and paused before answering. "There are still several hours before sunset." He spoke absently, as though he had forgotten Sara was there.

Sara got up from the mat and laid a hand on his shoulder. "I will go look for her. She can't be far."

She went up the hillside behind Ahaz's house, knowing that it was a favorite grazing place for the old ewe. She couldn't find the sheep, but she found several fresh tracks. Deciding to follow them, Sara wandered down a well-trod path that ended at the bottom of a hill. She could see the tracks cross over and begin to ascend on the other side. As she followed the trail, she lost track of time, not noticing that the sun was quickly descending to the horizon. She forgot everything in her fear for the ewe.

Coming upon a small pool of water, she could see where the ewe had stopped to drink. As she bent down to examine the tracks to find which direction the sheep had gone from here, she noticed another set of tracks. They looked like dog tracks, but larger. A shiver chased down her spine. Wolves.

Getting up quickly, she hurried in the direction of the tracks. It never occurred to her that her life might be in danger. Her thoughts were centered on little Nopet.

She came out on the edge of the hillside, looking down over a small valley. Rocks jutted precariously in several directions, making several ledges. Sara carefully went from ledge to ledge, looking over their sides. Her breath caught in her throat at the deep gorge that ran about three hundred feet below her. A rushing stream of water snaked off to the west, and as Sara followed it with her eyes, she noticed how far the sun had set.

Knowing that Antonius would probably be at her house by now, she got quickly to her feet. She glanced helplessly around, trying to decide what to do. She would just have to go back. Someone else would have to come look for Nopet. Probably the little ewe was already home, being cuddled by her worried owner.

She started to climb back down the way she had come when she heard a sound coming from her left. She froze, her heart beginning to thunder in panic. The sound came to her again. A soft bleating. She hurried towards the sound, her feet slipping and sliding on the rocks.

When she reached the area where she thought the sound had come from, she could see nothing. She waited, hoping to hear it again. After what seemed an eternity, she again heard the soft bleating coming from below her. Laying down, she leaned far out over the ledge. Below her, Nopet lay on the rocks, her head lifting pitifully as she cried for help.

"Oh," Sara murmured. "You poor little thing."

Now what was she to do? Even though the lamb was small, she was still fat and would be too heavy for Sara to lift off the rocks. She would have to go for help. As Sara turned to go back from the ledge, she could hear a cracking sound coming from beneath her. Her eyes opened wide in alarm, but before she could scramble to safety the ledge gave way, and Sara felt herself tumbling through space. A scream ripped from her throat, only to be silenced as her body hit the rocks below.

❧

"Antonius, if you love me, don't make me do this."

Antonius turned away from the tearful face of his sister. He was beginning to feel like a monster. "It's because I love you that I'm making you marry Flavius."

"I can't believe Flavius agreed to this," she murmured, almost to herself.

"Let's just say that I talked him into it. I can be most persuasive when I need to be," he told her, and she flinched at his arrogance.

"Oh, I know that," she told him angrily. "Sometimes you are like Satan incarnate."

"Satan?" He had never heard that term before.

"The evil one who controls the world," she explained.

Antonius felt as though he had just been sliced in his heart by a dagger. Could she really believe that of him? He was only doing what he thought best. He loved her and wanted to see her happy.

"I thought your Christian God controlled the world," he told her wryly, the hurt evident in his voice.

"In the end, He does. But Satan has control of everything evil. In the end, God will triumph over Satan, but in the meantime we must suffer with Satan's presence."

"How have you come to know so much in so little a time?" he demanded.

Diana dropped her head, refusing to answer.

"No matter," he told her firmly. "When you and Flavius are married, he will take you away from all of that. You will have children and learn to be a good Roman wife."

"Nothing you can do can take me away from the love of God," she answered him softly.

Frustrated, Antonius picked up his mantle. He struggled with something to say that would make her understand just how much Flavius and he loved her. "Tomorrow, Diana," he told her. "You will marry Flavius tomorrow. The arrangements have all been made."

He watched her for any sign that might show a softening in her attitude, but he found none. Sighing, he turned and left.

The sun was beginning to descend from the noon sky when he headed outside the city. Leaving Ephesus behind, he breathed deeply of the fresh air. Though Ephesus was beautiful, reputed to be second only to Rome, it was filled with the stench of rotting humanity. Having never considered himself a moral man before, he wondered at the change in his attitude.

He had never taken part in the city's wild orgies. In fact, he had allowed himself to feel somewhat superior to those who chose to participate. Now he realized that by condoning their acts, he was just as bad. Why had he not seen it before?

He had recently read the book of Hosea in his Jewish collection of scrolls. It appalled him that Hosea's God would command him to take an adulteress as a wife. But perhaps Hosea's people thought as little of adultery as did the Romans. He, on the other hand, would probably kill his wife if she did such a thing.

But Hosea's God had talked to him about the Israelites worshipping idols. He told them they would be destroyed because of it. He said an eagle was over the house of the Lord. Could He have meant Rome? Was Rome being used to punish the Israelites? And if so, would Rome then be destroyed by her own corruption?

He pulled his chariot to a halt in front of Jubal's house. Dismounting from it, he headed for the side of the house where Jubal had his shop. He knew they would be expecting him. He had sent word.

He found Jubal bent over the forge, his muscles rippling as he pumped the bellows. Antonius was impressed with the strength of the old man, though at fifty years of age he wasn't too old. Antonius fervently hoped he looked as good at that age. Many a legionnaire would envy this man his body.

"Shalom, Jubal," he told the man as he entered the shop.

Jubal turned his head at the Roman's entrance. No matter

how hard he tried, he couldn't help but like the young officer.

"Shalom."

"Is Sara ready to leave? My sister has missed her greatly."

Jubal turned back to the forge. "Sara isn't here right now. She went to visit Ahaz."

"I see. Do you mind if I sit?"

Jubal nodded towards the stool in the corner. Antonius made himself as comfortable as possible and struck up a conversation with the old Jew.

They talked about many things, finding much that they had in common. Antonius was surprised to see dusk beginning to settle on the land. He frowned. "Sara should have been back by now. It will be dark and too late to return to the city."

Jubal looked up from the forge, a sudden frown creasing his brow also. "You're right. Perhaps she came back and we didn't hear her."

He went to the connecting door and yelled for Abigail. She came quickly to his side, drying her hands on a towel.

"Has Sara returned?" Jubal asked, concern lacing his voice.

She looked past him in surprise at Antonius. "I thought perhaps they had already gone."

"Without saying goodbye?" Antonius asked sarcastically, getting rapidly to his feet.

Abigail and Jubal exchanged worried glances. Taking off his leather apron, Jubal turned to Antonius. "I'll go look for her."

"I'll go too," Antonius answered him, suddenly anxious.

Following Jubal to Ahaz's house, Antonius kept a constant watch along the road. When they reached the mud hut, Jubal pounded on the door.

"All right, all right. Don't break down my door."

Ahaz opened the door, squinting in the late afternoon light. "I thought you were Sara."

Jubal's face drained of color, and Antonius felt a tight knot of fear clutch at his heart.

"Where is Sara?" Jubal demanded.

"She went to find Nopet," the old man answered him worriedly. "But that was hours ago."

"Which way did she go?" Antonius demanded, and reined in his impatience when the old man squinted his eyes at him.

"Ah. The Roman," Ahaz wheezed. "Come to claim your property? More like come to find your master." The old man suddenly cackled with mirth, and Antonius frowned in annoyance. What was the old man talking about? It took a great deal of control to keep his hands from the old man's body.

"She went that way," Ahaz told them, pointing up the hill.

Antonius was already headed up the hill before Jubal caught up to him. "Tell me about this countryside," Antonius prodded.

"Up higher the hills become rocky. There's a deep gorge that has been carved out by a running stream. I don't think Sara has ever been this way before."

Jubal's worry mirrored his own. Antonius took a deep breath, climbing the hill quickly. When he reached the top he wasn't even breathing hard. Turning to Jubal, he found the old man had easily kept pace with him. Before long they found Sara's tracks.

"She's following an animal's tracks," Antonius said in surprise.

"Nopet is Ahaz's ewe."

"She's trying to find a stupid sheep!" Antonius was suddenly, inexplicably, filled with anger. He would throttle the girl with his bare hands when he found her.

"She's very special to Ahaz," Jubal answered him placatingly, recognizing the growing anger. Was he angry because he was worried, or because Sara was making him late?

"There are wolf tracks here also," Antonius told him worriedly.

"Then let's go. We haven't long until it will be too dark to see."

They followed the tracks, coming to the place where Sara had been laying on the ledge. The tracks ended abruptly, and there was no other sign.

Antonius was the first to hear the bleating of the ewe. Laying down, he leaned over the ledge. "I see the ewe," he told Jubal. "But I don't see. . .wait. . ."

Pushing himself carefully over the edge, Antonius gripped for handholds among the rocks. Slowly he lowered himself down as the last rays of light peeked over the mountains, leaving them in sudden darkness.

"Is she down there?" Jubal asked anxiously.

"Yes. She's unconscious. It looks like she hit her head on the rocks."

Antonius stared around him in the dark. He could barely make out the shapes of the hillside and could hear the water rushing below in the gorge.

"Jubal, there's no way to get her out of here without some rope. You need to go for help."

Jubal looked around him in the gathering darkness. The moon was a waxing gibbous in the sky, which afforded him some light, but not much. He wasn't sure he could find the same place in the dark.

"I'll be back as soon as I can," he told Antonius, turning to hurry down the hill.

Antonius knelt beside Sara. He could feel the stickiness in her hair and knew that it had to be blood. Taking off his mantle, he wrapped it gently around Sara as best he could without moving her. He was afraid to move her body without being able to see the extent of her injuries.

Sitting down beside her, he took her head gently into his lap. He brushed the dark strands from her eyes, his fingers softly tracing her cheekline. He felt along her shoulders and let his hand rest on her chest. The faint beating of her heart was reassuring, and he sighed with relief.

As he sat in the dark he could feel himself being watched. Glancing up, he could see yellow eyes peering at him from above.

"No, my friends," he said softly. "She belongs to me."

thirteen

Antonius didn't know how long he sat in the dark, cradling Sara's head in his lap, waiting for help. He petitioned every deity he was familiar with, and some he was not so familiar with. Finally he lifted his face to the night sky, glaring at the fiery stars over his head.

"All right, Sara's God, whoever You are. Wherever You are. She's in Your hands. She tells me You love her, and that nothing happens without Your will. What did she ever do to deserve this? Hasn't she been hurt enough? Some protector You are. Twice she has almost died."

He looked down at Sara's prostrate form and felt a lump forming in his throat. When had he begun to care so much? How had it happened? What was there about this girl, so unworldly and naive, so lacking in physical beauty, that had touched his heart?

Sighing, he leaned back against the rocks, unmindful of the sharp edges digging into his back. What was he to do now? He wanted Sara more than anything he had ever wanted in his life, but he knew she would never come to him willingly. Was that what made her so intriguing? Was it a desire to possess something that he couldn't have?

She stirred him physically like no woman ever had, yet he had barely touched her. They had exchanged a few kisses, nothing more, and yet he longed for more. The very scent of her roused thoughts in him that Sara would consider most inappropriate.

What was most unusual was the love of knowledge they both shared. He could talk to her for hours and know that she was just as desirous to learn more as he. Most of the women of his acquaintance were interested only in the games at the Coliseum or the theater or other such mindless occupations. Sara not only understood what he read from his scrolls, but could converse with him intelligently about them.

His hands stroked gently over her forehead. The blood seemed to have stopped flowing, and Antonius lifted his eyes heavenward again. "Thank You," he whispered, almost sure to which deity he was expressing his gratitude.

Sounds from above alerted him to the presence of the rescue crew. Torchlight brightened the area above his head, and Jubal's face peered at him from over the ledge.

"How is she?" He questioned anxiously.

"She's alive, more than that I don't know."

"I'm coming down."

A rope snapped out from the ledge and quickly unwound as it was lowered towards Antonius. Jubal followed the rope, his large form a suddenly reassuring presence to Antonius. When he reached Antonius' side, he bent down, taking Sara's hand into his. His hands swiftly scanned her body searching for other signs of injury. Finding none, he leaned back on his heels, sighing in relief.

"She hasn't awakened?"

"No," Antonius told him, gently lowering her head and getting to his feet.

"I've brought help. Let's get her out of here and back to Ahaz's," Jubal told him.

It didn't take long for them to get Sara to the top of the hill. Antonius and Jubal hurried down the hillside, not waiting to see if the men were able to get to Nopet. Antonius carried Sara in his arms, sweat beading his brow. Jubal was impressed with the young Roman's surefootedness even in these parts that were unknown to him.

Jubal touched the mezuzah on the doorpost, following

Antonius inside. The darkened interior was lit by one small lamp, the smoke drifting upwards to a crack in the ceiling. Ahaz rose from his mat, hurrying to their side.

"What happened?" he questioned.

Antonius and Jubal exchanged glances before Antonius strode across the room and laid Sara against the mat in the corner.

"Nopet fell over a ledge. Sara must have tried to help her," Jubal explained.

The old man's face paled as he hurried over to where Antonius had placed Sara. "And Nopet?"

"The men are trying to get her out. I don't know if she's been hurt or not," Jubal told him.

Kneeling beside Sara, Ahaz began to investigate her injuries. He lifted her eyelids gently before turning to Antonius. "She hasn't awakened at all?"

Antonius shook his head. "I'm not sure how long it's been since she fell, but the time I was with her she remained unconscious."

Ahaz glared at Antonius. "How is it, Roman, that ever since you have been around Sara, she seems to have become unusually accident prone?"

Rising to his feet, Antonius gave the old man a murderous look. "What are you saying, old man?"

Before Ahaz could answer, Sara moaned softly, turning her head slightly on the mat. Antonius knelt quickly by her side, stroking her dark hair gently from her cheeks and pushing it out of the way. Sara's eyes fluttered open and she gazed uncomprehendingly at Antonius.

"Antonius?"

Antonius. Not Tribune. Antonius smiled widely, his blue gaze focused on Sara's face as realization returned, and with it her usual reticence.

"What happened?" Sara frowned, trying to recall. "Nopet?"

Jubal came and bent down beside his daughter, taking her hand gently into his own. He grinned. "Perhaps next time Ahaz won't send a donkey to retrieve his lamb."

Sara smiled, trying to sit up. Her head began to reel, and the room started to spin. Moaning, she lay back on the mat.

, Antonius and Jubal focused their attention on Ahaz, their questions in their eyes. He was already preparing one of his concoctions and refused to look their way. Going to Sara, he bent and helped her to drink the brew. Within minutes she sighed, released from the pain.

"She hit her head or something hit her head. I don't know which. Regardless, the only injury I can find is to her head. Everything else seems to be fine."

"Aren't you going to give her something to make her sleep?" Antonius wanted to know, distressed that Sara would be suffering from the pain. Her face was so white and she lay quietly, her eyes opening and then drifting closed again.

Ahaz frowned at him. "No. She needs to be awake so that she doesn't drift into a deeper sleep than that from which she has already awakened. I have seen it happen before." Ahaz sat down next to Sara, settling himself comfortably on the mat. "We have a long night ahead of us. I need to make sure Sara stays awake."

Jubal was torn. He knew his wife would be frantic with worry. "I need to tell Abigail, but I will come back."

"I'll stay," Antonius told him firmly.

Although Sara was awake, she was in a surreal world with no thoughts of her own. Her mind drifted in and out of focus, and she felt unusually free from any worries. Even her father's anxious face caused nothing more than a slight feeling of regret.

"She's fortunate," Ahaz told them, "that she landed amongst the grass. It was thick enough to prevent her serious injury."

"God protected her," Jubal declared, a song of thanksgiving

rising to his lips.

Antonius felt the hair prickle on the back of his neck as Jubal recited words that Antonius had read among the Jewish scrolls. Words from their King David.

Jubal left shortly with a promise to return. Antonius made himself comfortable across from Ahaz, the only thing separating them being Sara's prostrate form. Antonius shifted uncomfortably as Ahaz continued to stare at him. The old man made him nervous. It was almost as though he could see inside his mind.

Ahaz hurried to the door when he heard a disturbance outside. Flinging open the portal, he let out a cry of joy as a sheep was thrust into his arms by its disgruntled rescuers. Thanking them profusely, Ahaz hurried to lay the sheep down and inspect it for injuries. Finding no serious ones, he began to scold the ewe gently even as she hurried to what was, Antonius supposed, her favorite corner. Only when the ewe had settled for the night did Ahaz turn again to Sara.

As Ahaz ministered to Sara, Antonius watched him warily. There was something on the old Jew's mind, and Antonius had no doubt Ahaz would come out with it sooner or later. Time passed slowly and Antonius chafed at the inactivity. He felt like he should do something.

"Relax, Roman. There's nothing we can do now except wait."

Antonius studied the man curiously. "You don't like me, do you?"

Ahaz snorted. "I suppose you're all right. For a Roman."

One dark eyebrow winged its way upward. "Such praise might go to my head. You should use it sparingly."

This was met by a cackle of laughter. Antonius recognized the wisdom behind those deep brown eyes and realized that he would like to have this man's respect.

Ahaz began to speak in Aramaic to Sara, trying to keep her

awake. He would switch periodically to Greek and then to Hebrew. Antonius recognized the tactic. Sara would have to try to concentrate on what he was saying which would help her to stay awake.

Antonius stared at Sara's pale face. When her eyes switched to him she smiled slightly, and Antonius felt his heart respond.

"You are so handsome," she whispered, and Antonius raised his eyebrows, his glance flicking to Ahaz.

"She's unaware of what she's saying. The drug I gave her confuses the mind, but relieves it of pain."

Antonius frowned. Her whispered words had filled him with happiness, but now he wasn't sure. What did she really think of him? Did she know how much he cared for her? Did she feel the same? She responded to his kisses, but that was only a physical reaction. Antonius knew he wanted more. Much more.

Smiling down into Sara's eyes, he decided to take a chance. "As you are beautiful," he told her softly, bending forward and touching his lips to hers. When he lifted his head, Sara reached her hand up and gently stroked her fingers down his cheek before letting her hand fall limply back to her side. Closing her eyes, she sighed softly. Antonius leaned back, content for the moment to leave things as they were.

Ahaz opened his mouth to speak, but was startled into silence when thundering hoofbeats passed the old hut. Antonius went to the door, recognizing the jingling of Roman cingulum as the horses went by. He opened the door quickly, but they were already rounding the bend. Frowning, he closed the door and returned to sit beside Sara. Although her eyes were dazed, they were focused on him.

What were Roman soldiers doing here and at this time of night? His eyes met those of Ahaz, and he saw the same question mirrored in their mysterious brown depths.

It was only moments later until they heard the horses returning. Jumping to his feet, Antonius reached the door just as the horses stopped outside. Before he could release the latch, someone started to pound furiously on the door.

Antonius flung the door open and stepped back in surprise when Flavius strode past him and into the room. Taking off his helmet, his gaze scanned the room before coming to rest on Antonius.

"I heard what happened. Will she be all right?" He nodded his head in Sara's direction.

"It would seem so." Antonius smiled wryly at Ahaz. "It appears that Jewish people have hard heads."

"Not any harder than your sister's," Flavius told him, clearly aggravated. There was something more in his attitude, and the smile left Antonius face.

"What's wrong?"

Sighing, Flavius pushed a hand through his dark hair. "Diana has disappeared."

The color drained from Antonius' face. "What do you mean she's disappeared?" he asked hoarsely, grabbing Flavius by the front of his cape.

Flavius pulled a small scroll from his belt. "She left this for you. She sent one to me also."

Antonius took the scroll and quickly unrolled it. His eyes scanned the brief message and Flavius could see them darken with his anger.

"What did yours say?" Antonius demanded.

Flavius rubbed a hand across his face, raising pain-filled eyes to Antonius. "She says that she cannot marry me and that it would be wrong before her God to do so. I have had soldiers discreetly searching the city for her all evening."

Antonius gritted his teeth in frustration. "How can she have disappeared? Where could she have gone? She wasn't well enough to have walked far."

Antonius thought back over the last two weeks. Diana had worked hard every day, practicing her walking. She had seemed almost driven in her efforts to get back on her feet. Now he understood why.

Antonius glanced back at Sara. He had to find Diana, but how could he leave Sara like this? Fear began to worm its way through him as he realized that he might possibly lose one or the other. Ahaz could see the indecision in Antonius' face and got up from his mat, ambling across the room until he reached Antonius' side.

"Sara will be fine," he told Antonius. "All she needs now is to rest. Her strength will return before many days, though her head may ache much longer."

Antonius sighed with relief. Going to Sara, he hunkered down beside her. "I will return for you in three days," he told her softly, letting his hand slide down her arm and squeeze her hand.

She watched him with unfocused eyes. Frowning, Antonius knew there was nothing more he could do here right now. He would find Diana and then come back for Sara. Getting quickly to his feet, Antonius strode past Flavius and out the door. Flavius turned swiftly on his heel and followed.

"I brought Orion from the old man's house."

Antonius nodded, swinging himself to the horse's back. "Let's go!" he commanded.

When they reached the villa, Antonius dismounted, handing the reins to Gallus. He turned to Flavius. "Have you no idea where she could be?"

Sliding off his own mount, Flavius shook his head. "I hoped that you would."

Antonius leaned against Orion. "By the gods, Flavius, what's happening? Everything is going to ruin. Nothing's the same."

Flavius felt Antonius' pain, realizing that in that way they had something to share. "I don't know, Antonius. Why would Diana run away? She said she loved me."

Antonius didn't answer. What could he say? He was only now beginning to understand himself. At first he had thought that Sara's God wasn't a very strong God since He hadn't been able to protect her from the things that were happening to her. After talking with Diana, he wondered if perhaps these things were caused by the one Diana called Satan instead. Perhaps this Satan was trying to destroy Sara and her family, and instead Sara's God had intervened on their behalf. He had witnessed some incredible things where Christians were concerned.

A sudden thought occurred to Antonius. "Do you have any idea where General Titus lives?" he asked.

Flavius looked surprised. "General Titus? I haven't heard his name mentioned in years. Why do you ask?"

"Come inside and I'll explain. Then we'll see if we can find him or one of these other Christians. Maybe Diana is hiding out with them."

❧

Antonius knocked at Jubal's door and waited. Moments later the door opened, and Abigail faced him. She stood back wordlessly and waited for him to pass.

Sara was sitting by the counter in the kitchen, slicing cucumbers into a bowl. She looked up, her face suffusing with color.

"Tribune. I'll only be a moment." She placed the knife on the counter and got to her feet.

"Take your time."

Antonius watched her gather her things together, going to her mother and hugging her. A gash on her forehead was surrounded by a huge purple bruise, and Antonius winced involuntarily.

"Are you sure you are recovered?"

Sara came to stand before Antonius, her head bowed. "Yes, Tribune."

Antonius felt irritation rising in him. She had called him Antonius before, had even told him he was handsome, now here she was back to calling him Tribune. Perhaps it was her mother's presence, or perhaps she had been told of her words to him and now was embarrassed by them.

He handed her into the chariot as Jubal came from the side of the house. Jubal's eyes went from one to the other before coming back to Sara. "Take care, Sara."

She smiled back at him. "And you."

Antonius walked back to Jubal and handed him a small leather pouch. Jubal looked at him questioningly even as his hand reached for it.

"For you," Antonius told him before turning on his heel and rejoining Sara in the chariot. Wrapping his arms securely around her, he lifted the reins, slapping them against the horse.

Sara felt almost glad to be returning. She had missed Diana, but she had missed Antonius more. She could feel his tenseness and knew that something was wrong. He had been almost cold. Distant. Was it something she had done?

"Diana is missing," he told her without emotion.

Turning her head sharply, Sara stared at him in surprise. "How? When?"

"The day I came to get you. You know nothing of this?" His blue eyes showed his uncertainty.

She shook her head. "No, Tribune." Turning back to the front of the chariot, Sara offered a silent prayer for Diana's safety. She turned back to Antonius.

"Have you looked for her?" she asked, and then realized what a foolish question that was.

"Sara," Antonius told her softly. "Diana ran away from marrying Flavius."

"Oh." Sara saw they were rapidly approaching the city, and her mind was trying to think quickly what to do. Had Diana gone to fellow Christians to hide out? They would have understood her plight and been willing to help her. Antonius must be hurting abominably. He loved Diana. But then why would he try to force her into marriage? It didn't make sense.

When they arrived at the villa, Antonius handed her down. "You are free to do as you please until I can find Diana. I'll be in the bibliotheca if you need me."

Turning, he strode away. Sara watched him go with some misgiving. He was hurt, but he was angry too. She went inside only to find the whole villa in a state of mourning. Everyone loved Diana, and everyone was concerned.

Deciding to see if what she had supposed was correct, Sara took a cape and slipped out the side gate. So intent was she on her mission that she failed to notice the figure that slipped out behind her. Hurrying through the streets, she came to the rundown section of the city. She went to the apartment that she had been to so many times with Decimus. Knocking gently, the door opened and she went inside.

"Sara!" Diana ran to her, throwing her arms around Sara and hugging her tightly. Tears flowed freely from both of their faces.

"Diana! Antonius is worried about you."

Diana drew back slightly, her eyes filling again with tears. "I know. I'm sorry, but I had to leave. I couldn't go through with it."

"What happened? I knew you were supposed to marry Flavius, but I didn't think you would run away."

Taking her by the hand, Diana pulled her over and had Sara sit near the window. Facing the room, Sara smiled at General Titus and his wife, Callista.

"Welcome, Sara," General Titus told her, handing her a cup of posca. Sara took the watered wine and smiled her thanks, turning back to Diana.

"You have been here all this time?"

Diana nodded, dropping her hands to her lap. "Antonius must want to kill me."

Sara sighed. "I don't know about that, but when he brought me home today he was very quiet. More so than usual."

Diana and Sara exchanged stories when General Titus and his wife left the room. That Diana was miserable was obvious, though she tried not to show it. Her lovely blue eyes were dulled with worry. Sara wondered why Antonius had sent her away when he was planning Diana's wedding. Did he think she would try to stop it?

Someone knocked on the door and Callista went to answer it. Sara and Diana smiled at each other. General Titus was a kind and helpful man. Many people found their way to his door and he helped them all, even if it meant giving them his last denarii. Diana had been only one of many.

Callista opened the door, her breath drawing in sharply in surprise. Diana and Sara rose quickly to their feet, only to find themselves staring into Antonius' cold blue eyes. Sara realized then that he must have followed her here. Flavius stood to his side and slightly behind him. Seeing Diana, he pushed past Antonius and came to stand before her.

"Why?"

The one word held such a wealth of hurt that Sara felt her throat close tightly. She looked past Flavius to Antonius. He was so unmoving, his face revealing nothing.

General Titus came back into the room, stopping in mid-stride. His eyes widened in surprise and then filled with welcome. "Antonius! It's been years!"

Antonius felt some of his anger evaporate. Christian or no, this man had at one time been like a father to him, and Antonius had loved and respected him. Glancing around at the tenement apartment, clean but so obviously a hovel,

Antonius felt Rome's betrayal of one of her best, due to this same pagan religion that Sara embraced.

"General Titus," he acknowledged. "I've come to fetch my sister."

There was silence in the room until Diana finally broke it. "I'll get my things," she said softly to no one in particular.

"I'll come with you." Flavius followed her from the room.

Feeling uncomfortable, Sara turned away from Antonius' dark perusal. She went to Callista and hugged her. "Thank you." Looking into her eyes, Callista knew that she wanted to say more, but something held her back. She gazed over Sara's shoulder at Antonius and raised her brows, but said nothing. Turning to her husband, she said, "Should you not offer Antonius some posca?"

"Thank you, but I haven't time," he told her softly.

Callista stared at him, her lips tilting up in humor. "It may be some time before your sister returns," she told him.

Antonius looked over her shoulder to the hallway where his sister and Flavius had disappeared. He could hear what amounted to a heated argument, and his eyes came back to Callista's face. His lips quirked in humor. "You could be right."

"Come in then, and have a seat, boy," the general told him. "We have a lot of catching up to do."

Antonius sat in the seat indicated, motioning for Sara to sit beside him. Reluctantly, Sara did as she was bidden. She was very aware of Antonius and the arm he draped over the couch behind her.

"I understand you've become a Christian?" Antonius cut right to the heart of the matter. He respected this man more than he had any other, save his father. His question invited an explanation.

General Titus explained how his conversion had come about. His eyes gleamed intensely as he focused his attention on Antonius. "I have never seen anything like it before or since. The sun refused to shine for three hours. The earth shook and rocks were split apart everywhere."

The words so softly spoken caused a chill to race down Antonius' spine. If anyone else had told him such a thing he would have scoffed, but not this man. Antonius knew him too well.

"You were in Jerusalem when this happened?"

"Yes. I was there with my soldiers to help still the threat of insurrection. But God had other plans for my life."

"Does this God have a name?" Antonius inquired, impressed despite himself.

"Some call him Jehovah. Some El Shaddai. There are many names for Him," the general told him.

"Like Zeus and Jupiter?" Antonius asked skeptically.

General Titus laughed. "No, my friend. Each of His names means something special in Greek, Aramaic and Hebrew. His names explain who He is at certain times. Sometimes He's the Father chastising His children, sometimes the Judge passing sentence."

Antonius nodded in understanding. "I see."

Sara looked at him in surprise, because it sounded as though he really did understand. Her heart began to beat harder. Could he possibly understand it all? *Please, God, let him believe.*

Diana and Flavius entered the room, and Antonius noted the defeat etched across his friend's face, his shoulders slumped in dejection. Diana was being stubborn, no doubt. His lips thinned in anger. He would handle this matter at home.

Getting to his feet, Antonius pulled Sara swiftly to hers. Placing a hand on the small of her back, he propelled her towards the door.

Diana turned at the door, tears in her eyes. "Thank you for taking me in. May God bless you." Turning, she fled outside.

As the general and his wife watched the four walk away, General Titus turned to his wife. "Come, Callista. I think we have some heavy praying to do."

fourteen

Antonius watched his sister and Flavius out the window of the bibliotheca, tempted to intervene. The same scenario had been performed for the last two weeks. Everyday, Flavius came to see Diana, and within a short period of time they were in a heated argument, then Flavius would leave, only to return the next day and try again.

Shaking his head, Antonius decided not to interfere. This was something they had to work out for themselves. After talking with Diana, Antonius realized how distraught she was over the thought of marrying a man who didn't share her faith. He had finally granted permission for her to decline the marriage. It had been hard to do. Flavius had been extremely hurt. He had refused to give up, and Diana loved him enough to try to win him to her way of thinking.

Diana was vociferously arguing her cause when Flavius suddenly swooped forward and kissed her on her surprised mouth. Color flew to Diana's cheeks, and Antonius had to grin. *Atta boy, Flavius. Keep her off balance.*

Antonius turned at a sound from the doorway. Sara stopped on the threshold and stared at him questioningly. He felt his heart squeeze within him. This was something else that was going to be hard to do.

"You wished to see me, Tribune?"

"Come in, Sara." Antonius motioned her forward. "There's something I need to discuss with you." His eyes roved over her, taking in the colorful yellow tunic she wore. She looked like a butterfly in the sunshine.

Sara felt her heart start to pound. What had she done to

cause such a look on Antonius' face? Something was terribly wrong and she had no idea what it could possibly be.

Antonius couldn't bring himself to look Sara in the face, so he busied himself rolling up scrolls and putting them away in their cubicles. With his back to her, he leaned heavily against the carved desk. "Sara," he began reluctantly, and Sara became more concerned. She had never seen him so unsure of himself.

Sighing, he turned to face her, leaning back against the desk. "I've made inquiries to find out about your brother, Dathan. I had it in mind to have him set free."

A smile spread across Sara's face at the news, her heart suddenly filled with joy. Dathan coming home! The smile left her face as rapidly as it came. Antonius didn't look pleased at all. "You couldn't find him?" she asked hesitantly.

His eyes met hers briefly and quickly flicked away. He motioned her to a seat, coming to kneel in front of her when she slowly lowered herself into it.

Antonius licked suddenly dry lips, taking one of Sara's hands into his own. He began to absently stroke her wrist with his fingers, not realizing the effect he was having on her.

"I only know of one way to tell you this," he told her firmly, his eyes fully meeting hers for the first time.

"Dathan is dead," he told her softly, his throat closing around the words. He felt her begin to tremble, her eyes growing wide with horror. Slowly she shook her head from side to side.

"No! It can't be!"

Sara's mind began to whirl with her confusing thoughts. Dathan dead. How was it possible? Surely God had a purpose for his life. He couldn't die this young, he just couldn't. Feelings of guilt overwhelmed her. She hadn't been the kind of sister she should have been, and truth to tell, she had loved Decimus more than her own brother.

Now she could never make it up to him, never ask his forgiveness. She felt somehow to blame. Staring into the intense blue eyes in front of her, she felt her anger begin to boil. Hadn't she told Antonius that Dathan was just a boy? He couldn't be expected to survive such harsh conditions as the galleys.

Black anger clouded her reasoning as she continued to stare at Antonius. He was to blame. He was the one who had put these things into motion and brought such a disaster upon her brother.

"It's your fault," she told him tonelessly.

Antonius released her hands, drawing back at the pain she inflicted with her words. He had already fought with his own feelings of guilt, his own self-condemnation. But there was more that Sara needed to know. There was more to the story.

"Sara."

"No!" Sara jumped to her feet, almost knocking him to the floor where he was still kneeling. When he reached out to her, she drew back sharply and stared at him with loathing. "You killed him. You murdered him!"

"Enough!"

"I hate you!" she gritted through clenched teeth.

Sara was beyond reasoning, beyond fear of retribution. Lifting her hand, she violated all the laws of Rome and struck her master a resounding blow across the cheek. Turning, she fled from the room.

Antonius stared after her in surprise, his hand covering his cheek, where a red mark was beginning to show. By all rights, Sara had forfeited her life with such an action. He could have her fed to the lions in the arena, or even crucified her if he so chose. He shuddered at such a possibility.

Although he was angry at Sara's refusal to listen to his explanation, he understood her feelings. She had every right to accuse him. He hadn't given any consideration to anyone's feelings when he had taken Sara from her home and sent Dathan to the galleys. He hadn't cared who he had hurt as long as he got his way. Just like Rome. The words echoed in his mind and left him no peace. He would give Sara time to recover and then he would try again.

❧

Sara paused outside the bibliotheca, suppressing the shudder that ran through her. Antonius had demanded her presence and she thought she knew why. She had been foolish to slap him, and her rash action may have cost her her life. Taking a deep breath, she entered the room.

She was surprised to see Diana standing next to the desk where Antonius sat, her eyes full of compassion. Sara walked over and stood in front of Antonius, her head bowed respectfully.

Leaning across the table, Antonius laid a scroll in front of Sara. "Take it," he commanded, remembering another time.

Sara lifted her eyes to his and saw his pain reflected there. What had he to be hurt about? Thinking the scroll her death sentence, her fingers trembled as they reached forward and clasped the document.

"Antonius is giving you your freedom, Sara," Diana told her joyfully. "I'm going to miss you something fierce, but what he's doing is right."

Sara swallowed the knot in her throat. She didn't care that he was freeing her, or even that she wasn't to be punished for her actions earlier. Only one thought stood out clearly in her mind. He was sending her away.

Diana wrapped Sara gently in her arms and hugged her close. "We won't say goodbye, because I intend to see you again every time I get the chance. You must come to my wedding, also."

Looking up, Sara questioned Diana with her eyes. Color

filled Diana's cheeks and made her look more beautiful than ever.

"Flavius is coming around to my way of thinking. It may take some time, but I won't give up. God is supreme and His Word won't come back empty, so Flavius doesn't stand a chance. When that happens. . .then we'll be married," Diana finished softly.

Antonius got to his feet and came around the desk to stand beside them. He reached out a hand, but let it drop to his side.

"Get your things together. We'll leave for your home within the hour."

Confused, Sara turned away. She had told him she hated him and had slapped his face. She had blamed him for the death of her brother and called him a murderer. And he was giving her her freedom. She had expected to be punished and instead had been rewarded. Isn't that what was known as grace?

Heart breaking, Sara gathered her things together while Diana chatted to her. What did she expect? She had been a servant, nothing more. She had been wrong when she thought Antonius cared for her. Maybe he had, just a little, but she had destroyed that with her thoughtless words.

Antonius helped Sara into the chariot after she and Diana hugged each other, clinging together as friends. He wrapped his arms firmly around her, taking up the reins.

"I'll miss you," Diana yelled as they drove away.

Tears that had been held back now struggled for release. Believing herself unobserved, Sara let them trickle in masses down her cheeks. She should be glad she was going home, and in a way she was, but her heart felt torn apart by her confusing feelings regarding Antonius. She blamed him for the death of her brother, and yet she couldn't resolve that with the man she had come to know and love.

Antonius watched the tears wending their way down Sara's cheeks and felt his chest constrict painfully. He wanted to take her in his arms and hold her close, begging her forgiveness. But now wasn't the time or the place, and he had things to settle with her parents. He prayed that they would listen before condemning him.

They reached Sara's house as the sun was beginning to set. Lifting her down from the chariot, Antonius watched as she walked away, head held high. A smile twitched his lips. Stubborn to the end.

Antonius followed her into the house, knowing that Jubal would be through with his business for the day and that he would be preparing for supper.

Abigail and Jubal rose to their feet in surprise, Abigail's eyes locked onto her daughter's distressed face. Raising her eyebrows, she sought the reason from Antonius.

"I must speak with you," he told them quietly, while Sara set about putting her things away. Antonius followed her with his eyes, wanting to reach out to her. Comfort her.

"Have a seat," Jubal told him, "and share our supper."

"I need to get some water," Sara told them desperately and fled out the door. Antonius started to rise and go after her, but realized her parents were waiting. Lowering himself back to the mat, he sighed heavily.

Sara returned to find her mother in tears, her father preparing to come after her, and Antonius gone. She had been gone several hours and darkness had descended, but she couldn't bring herself to come back. She had lain on the grass watching the stars appear and wondering at God's will for their lives. *Oh Dathan, Dathan. Are you with God?* Remembering his life, she doubted it and felt even more sorrow.

Laying the empty water skin on the table, Sara went to her mother and tried to comfort her, only to realize that she was not wailing as the Jewish people normally did for their dead.

Though her eyes were filled with tears, there was joy and acceptance there also. Perplexed, she turned to her father.

"Antonius told us that you didn't let him explain about your brother's death," he told her sorrowfully. "Perhaps you should have listened."

"Listened! What could he say that could bring Dathan back? What could he say that would take away his guilt in this matter?"

"Dathan is with God," her father told her quietly, and she curled her hands into fists at her sides.

"How can you say that? You know how he lived!"

"But I also know how he died," he told her angrily, "and if you would listen, you would see the hand of God in all of this."

Her father watched her struggling to comprehend his attitude and realized that he had failed her in this regard. He should have trusted God and not blamed the Roman for his son's own foolishness. "Sit down, Sara," he commanded quietly.

Sara sat on the mat next to the table where Antonius had been, the food forgotten. She picked up a date and began to twirl it in her fingers. Her father looked tired, but somehow jubilant. She had missed something by staying away. Something important.

Her father sat across from her, crossing his legs. He began to explain to her what Antonius had told him about Dathan's death.

Dathan had been assigned to the galleys of a Roman warship. There had been ninety-nine other rowers, besides himself and the drummer. When the warship had gone to the aid of a grain ship coming from Alexandria that was being attacked by pirates, a fierce battle had ensued. The warship had rammed the pirate ship, but in doing so had busted open its own hull, causing the Mediterranean to rush in. Although

Dathan had been one of the first freed, he had refused to leave without helping the others. He had gone down with the warship, still trying to free the other slaves.

Tears poured freely down Sara's face, and she was filled with an acute pride in her brother. Her mother was sobbing softly in the kitchen area as she put away the supper dishes.

"I'm proud to know that he would die to save others," she told her father softly. "But what of repentance?"

Jubal smiled at his daughter. "One of the slaves told Antonius when he was questioned that shortly after Dathan arrived, he started talking to them about God's love. He sang hymns while he rowed and praised God whenever he had the chance. Many of the slaves who died with the ship, died in the Lord, thanks to Dathan. He. . ." Jubal choked on the words and Sara went swiftly to him.

"It's all right, father."

Jubal hugged his daughter close, burying his face in her neck. He sobbed quietly for the loss of his only son.

"I don't know how or why Dathan repented, but God has allowed us to know that he did." Jubal pulled back from his daughter and looked seriously into her face. "And I will thank God every day for sending the Roman into our lives."

Sara felt her heart lurch at his words. She had blamed Antonius for her brother's death, when in all probability he had saved his eternal life. What would have happened if Dathan had continued on the path he had chosen? Thank God for Antonius' wisdom. Thank God for Antonius' heart. Now how was she ever going to be able to apologize and ask forgiveness?

❧

Sara sat alone in the copse in the wood, knees drawn up under her chin. She was so still that a fallow deer entered the wood without suspecting her presence. She smiled slightly.

It had been a long time since she had come to her favorite

spot. Her thinking spot. Not since the accident with Antonius. Sighing, Sara closed her eyes and brought his image to her mind, but the only image she had was of blue eyes filled with hurt and pain. It had been several weeks, and still the memory wouldn't go away. When she opened her eyes again, he was standing not more than twenty feet away. Thinking she was seeing a vision, she hastily closed her eyes and opened them again.

He was still standing there, more handsome than ever. His short white tunic was trimmed with purple, the color of the aristocracy, and his leather belt emphasized the leanness of his waist.

"I thought I might find you here," he told her quietly. She looked for some kind of emotion, but found nothing. Why was he here?

He walked over and sat down on the log next to her. Though he didn't look at her or touch her, still she felt herself firmly attached to his presence.

They didn't speak for several minutes, each concerned with their own thoughts. It was Sara who finally made the first move towards reconciliation.

"I was hoping I'd see you again and have the chance to apologize. To ask your forgiveness."

He looked at her then, his face registering his surprise. "You have nothing to apologize for. I'm the one who should be apologizing." He leaned his head forward, pushing the palms of his hands against his eyes. "Can you ever forgive me?"

Sara's heart went out to him. She could see now what she hadn't seen at a distance. Tired lines radiated out from around his eyes, and he was thinner than before. His face was almost haggard.

"I forgave you a long time ago," she told him softly. "My father told me about Dathan. I'm sorry I misjudged you.

Please forgive me for the awful things I said. I let my Lord down terribly in my words and my actions."

Antonius let out his breath, turning to face her. "I think you're more like Jesus than you know," he replied, and smiled at Sara's astonished reaction. His smile faded as he continued to stare at her, his eyes resting on her lips. Suddenly he jumped to his feet and began pacing.

"Zeus! With my arrogance it's a wonder God didn't strike me down dead. What I wanted I took." He looked down at her and his voice quieted. "Even you."

Sara looked away from him. "My parents have helped me to remember that everything that happened was by God's will. I have a tendency to forget that."

Antonius kneeled in front of her, placing a hand on each side of her on the log. He was so close that Sara could smell the fragrance of sandalwood he used after his baths. She tried to move away, but there was no place to go.

He leaned forward until his lips were mere inches from her own. "As long as you don't forget me," he told her softly, huskily.

Sara's heart pounded furiously. What was he trying to say? Did he care for her after all, or was he trying to assuage his feelings of guilt?

"I could never forget you," she answered him softly.

A fire seemed to ignite behind his eyes, and she thought he was going to kiss her. Instead he leaned back, a dubious expression crossing his face.

"And what exactly do you remember?" he asked doubtfully.

Sara's lips twitched. "I remember a man who loved his sister so much he would do anything for her. I remember a man who tried to help his friend find happiness with the woman he loved. I remember a man who freed my parents when he had no need," she finished softly. "Why didn't you tell me?"

He turned his face away, embarrassed, but Sara reached out and gently turned it back so she could see his eyes. His hand went up to cover hers, holding it in place against his cheek.

"I wanted to, but I didn't want you to feel beholden to me."

Sara's forehead creased in a frown. "I don't understand."

Letting go of her hand, Antonius rose to his feet, pulling Sara up and into his arms. He bent forward, kissing her gently on the nose.

"I love you, Sara," he told her. "I want to marry you, but I didn't want you to marry me because you felt you owed me. I freed you for the same reason. I wanted to make sure that what I felt for you was real, not just something physical whenever I was around you."

Sara stared up at him, her mouth open in surprise. How many times had she dreamed those words, prayed for this moment. She loved Antonius with all of her heart, but she couldn't marry him. Only in her dreams, her fantasies, but never for real. Diana realized the danger and stood firm against the temptation; how could Sara do less?

She tried to pull away, but Antonius wouldn't let her. Did he know that just by holding her he could cloud her thinking? Every time it had been harder and harder to deny him.

"I can't marry you, Antonius," she groaned softly.

His brow furrowed and his eyes lit with anger. "What do you mean, you can't marry me? Are you trying to tell me you don't love me? Because if you are, I don't believe you."

Swooping down, he kissed her passionately and felt her body melt into his embrace. Getting no resistance, Antonius gentled his kisses, reveling in Sara's response. He lifted his lips slowly from hers and stared intently into her eyes.

"Now tell me you don't love me."

Sara's body was trembling all over. Her legs would not support her and if not for Antonius' arms, she would have found herself on the ground. She leaned her forehead against his chest and could feel his heart pounding with a rhythm to match her own.

"I don't deny that I love you." Her voice was muffled against his tunic, and Antonius had to strain to hear her. "But I can't marry you."

Realizing she meant what she said, Antonius jerked her back to face him. His face colored angrily and his fingers bit into her arms.

"By the gods! You can't mean it!" He shook her none too gently. "Why?"

Sara saw the pain in his eyes and her own filled with tears. "I can't marry you for the same reason Diana wouldn't marry Flavius. You're not a Christian."

Dawning comprehension brought a sparkle to Antonius' eyes, and his fingers relaxed their hold. "Is that the only reason?" he wanted to know, and Sara nodded her head.

"And what if I tell you that Flavius and Diana are to be married in three weeks?"

Sara jerked her head up in surprise. Had Diana given in after all? Had the temptation been too great? Poor Diana. She tried to push out of Antonius' hold, but he still refused to let her go. There was laughter in his eyes, and Sara felt her temper begin to rise.

"I'm not Diana. I won't marry a man unless he's a Christian."

"Then marry me," Antonius demanded softly.

Ceasing her struggles, Sara stared at him in amazement. "You?"

"Yes, me." He saw the doubt filling her eyes, and he began to shake his head. "No, Sara. Not just to marry you. I've learned a lot about Jesus in the last few months. Before, He was just a story about an insurrectionist. Now I know the truth. I've spoken to many people who witnessed His death, including General Titus, and I can't doubt their words." He rubbed his finger gently against her cheek, across her nose and up her other cheek. "But even more than that, I've seen what He can do in someone's life after His death. Take Diana, for instance."

Sara felt as if her heart would burst with happiness. Oh, God had truly blessed her life. Now she understood what the Apostle Paul had meant when he said that all things worked together for the good for those who loved God.

"Beloved," Antonius whispered, pulling her more firmly into his embrace. "Marry me."

Eyes shining, Sara shyly lifted her lips to his. Antonius marveled at her sweetness and how a few words had changed her from a fighting vixen to a soft lamb. His body responded to her show of love and his kiss deepened. For the first time, Antonius felt like he had come home, welcomed by the one God had chosen for him from the beginning. He was awed by God's patience, His goodness and His love.

Things would not be easy, but with God's help all things were possible. Antonius reached for Sara's hand, clasping it firmly in his own. He smiled down into her face, kissing her softly on her lips, then turning, they walked out of the forest together.

epilogue

Sara stared out her bedroom window at the sun rising over Ephesus. The beautiful columns of the Artemesion shone whitely against the morning sun, its pink rays spreading their fingers across the sleepy city.

How could someplace so beautiful be so full of evil? Everywhere, Satan had a grip on this city. A citizenry that prided themselves on their tolerance of other religions and their belief that they were more civilized than other races, and yet they sent hundreds to die in the arenas for their amusement.

Antonius came up behind her, sliding his arms around her already swollen waist. She sighed as he began to nibble on her earlobe and leaned back against him.

"Couldn't you sleep?"

Sara shook her head. "I'm worried, Antonius."

He sighed heavily. "As am I. Now that Nero is Caesar, I think things are going to become much worse for the Christians."

"What can we do?"

Antonius turned her in his arms, kissing her lightly on the nose. "I think it's time that I take you and the baby to safety. When things change, maybe we can come back."

Sara felt the beginnings of real fear. "But where can we go?"

"I thought we might go to Alexandria, in Egypt."

Sara's mouth dropped open. "So far?"

"That's the point, beloved," he told her patiently. "Although it is an important city, it's far enough from Rome to be relatively safe. Your parents have agreed to come with us."

Smiling brightly, Sara hugged him. "How did you manage that?"

Antonius laughed. "I reminded Jubal how close Alexandria is to Jerusalem. Your father has a desire to see his home again."

Suddenly sobering, Sara turned back to the window. "Before now, the only people who persecuted Christians were the Jews. Now, it seems everyone is against us. Why? We preach nothing but peace and love. How can anyone hate those things?"

Resting his chin against the top of her head, Antonius sighed. "People don't want to be reminded of their sins. They want life to accept them as they are, no matter how depraved they might be."

"Perhaps God intends us to spread the Word. If not for this persecution, wouldn't you be content to remain safely here in Ephesus?"

Antonius agreed. "I don't know why these things have to happen. I don't know why a good man like General Titus and his wife Callista had to be slaughtered in the arena. I only know that we have to trust in God."

"And Diana?"

"She and Flavius have agreed to come, also."

"Thank God," Sara sighed in relief.

As the sun rose brightly in the morning sky, Antonius made arrangements for his family to leave Ephesus. They would travel a long way and become pilgrims in a strange land, but the Lord would always be with them.

Not long after they left Ephesus, Rome burned and along with it much of what was still human and moral. Nero chose to blame the Christians, though there were those who said it was actually Nero himself who ordered the destruction.

Far away in the land of Alexandria, Sara gave birth to a son and named him Zephaniah, because God had protected him from the evil and destruction of Rome.

A Letter To Our Readers

Dear Reader:

In order that we might better contribute to your reading enjoyment, we would appreciate your taking a few minutes to respond to the following questions. When completed, please return to the following:

Rebecca Germany, Managing Editor
Heartsong Presents
P.O. Box 719
Uhrichsville, Ohio 44683

1. Did you enjoy reading *The Eagle and the Lamb*?
   ❏ Very much. I would like to see more books
      by this author!
   ❏ Moderately
      I would have enjoyed it more if _____

   _____

2. Are you a member of **Heartsong Presents**? ❏ Yes ❏ No
   If no, where did you purchase this book? _____

   _____

3. What influenced your decision to purchase this
   book? (Check those that apply.)

   ❏ Cover   ❏ Back cover copy

   ❏ Title   ❏ Friends

   ❏ Publicity   ❏ Other _____

4. How would you rate, on a scale from 1 (poor) to 5
   (superior), the cover design? _____

5. On a scale from 1 (poor) to 10 (superior), please rate the following elements.

    ___ Heroine   ___ Plot

    ___ Hero   ___ Inspirational theme

    ___ Setting   ___ Secondary characters

6. What settings would you like to see covered in **Heartsong Presents** books?_____

_____

_____

7. What are some inspirational themes you would like to see treated in future books?_____

_____

_____

8. Would you be interested in reading other **Heartsong Presents** titles?   ❑ Yes   ❑ No

9. Please check your age range:
  ❑ Under 18   ❑ 18-24   ❑ 25-34
  ❑ 35-45   ❑ 46-55   ❑ Over 55

10. How many hours per week do you read? _____

Name _____

Occupation _____

Address _____

City_____ State_____ Zip _____

Romance is Back
"Inn" Style!

From New England to Hawaii and Canada to the Caribbean, *The Christian Bed & Breakfast Directory* has a romantic home-away-from-home waiting for your pleasure. The 1997-98 edition of the directory includes over 1,400 inns. Choose from secluded cabins, beachfront bungalows, historical mansion suites, and much more.

Relevant information about bed and breakfast establishments and country inns is included, inns that are eager to host Christian travelers like you. You'll find descriptions of the inns and accommodation details, telephone numbers and rates, credit card information, and surrounding attractions that satisfy a variety of interests and ages. Maps are also included to help you plan a wonderful romantic getaway.

608 pages; paperbound; 5" x 8"

Send to: Heartsong Presents Reader's Service
P.O. Box 719
Uhrichsville, Ohio 44683

Please send me _____ copies of *The Christian Bed & Breakfast Directory* at **$4.97 each**. I am enclosing $_____ (please add $1.00 to cover postage and handling per order. OH add 6.25% tax. NJ add 6% tax.). Send check or money order, no cash or C.O.D.s, please. **To place a credit card order, call 1-800-847-8270.**

NAME _____

ADDRESS _____

CITY/STATE _____ ZIP _____

·······Hearts♥ng ·······

HEARTSONG PRESENTS TITLES AVAILABLE NOW:

(If ordering from this page, please remember to include it with the order form.)

••••••• **Presents** •••••••

Great Inspirational Romance at a Great Price!

Heartsong Presents books are inspirational romances in contemporary and historical settings, designed to give you an enjoyable, spirit-lifting reading experience. You can choose wonderfully written titles from some of today's best authors like Peggy Darty, Tracie J. Peterson, Colleen L. Reece, Lauraine Snelling, and many others.

When ordering quantities less than twelve, above titles are $2.95 each.

SEND TO: Heartsong Presents Reader's Service
P.O. Box 719, Uhrichsville, Ohio 44683

Please send me the items checked above. I am enclosing $_____.
(please add $1.00 to cover postage per order. OH add 6.25% tax. NJ add 6%). Send check or money order, no cash or C.O.D.s, please.
To place a credit card order, call 1-800-847-8270.

NAME _____

ADDRESS _____

CITY/STATE_____ ZIP _____

HPS 1-97

Heart♥ng Presents
Love Stories Are Rated G!

That's for godly, gratifying, and of course, great! If you love a thrilling love story, but don't appreciate the sordidness of some popular paperback romances, **Heartsong Presents** is for you. In fact, **Heartsong Presents** is the *only inspirational romance book club*, the only one featuring love stories where Christian faith is the primary ingredient in a marriage relationship.

Sign up today to receive your first set of four, never before published Christian romances. Send no money now; you will receive a bill with the first shipment. You may cancel at any time without obligation, and if you aren't completely satisfied with any selection, you may return the books for an immediate refund!

Imagine. . .four new romances every four weeks—two historical, two contemporary—with men and women like you who long to meet the one God has chosen as the love of their lives. . .all for the low price of $9.97 postpaid.

To join, simply complete the coupon below and mail to the address provided. **Heartsong Presents** romances are rated G for another reason: They'll arrive *Godspeed!*